ADAM'S APPLES

Dream Doors Adventures Book 1

DOUGLAS HIRT
TERRY JAMES

Adam's Apples
Dream Doors Adventures Book 1
Douglas Hirt
Terry James

Paperback Edition

CKN Christian Publishing
An Imprint of Wolfpack Publishing
6032 Wheat Penny Avenue
Las Vegas, NV 89122

ISBN: 978-1-64119-160-9

ADAM'S APPLES

The Kingdom, 100 M.R.

ONE HUNDRED YEARS have passed since New Eden began.

Glorainia, the Kingdom city of New Eden, shines down upon the rainbow land that curves across the golden horizon. Sparks of beautifully colored lights fire from the glistening walls of the magnificent temple where the Great King dwells.

The Great King lives among the Edons, loving and caring for them – each and every one. His love desires that all obey, but few people do not want to obey. The Great King is perfect in his way.

New Eden time is changed completely from the Trouble Time and the Before Time. Death, disease, war and all the terrible things of the ages gone by now are but faded memories. The evols, locked away in the caverns deep within New Eden, no more do their mischief.

Bountiful fruit trees line the streets of Glorainia. Brightons and Lightons move among the Glorainians and all Edons everywhere. It is a time of wonders and adventures and much, much happiness.

Chapter 1

MEMORIES OF THE BEFORE TIME FADED WITH EACH bursting dawn. Sights and sounds and smells filled Glorainia with fragrances of all things made new. Trees as tall as trees could ever be ringed the Middle Land street called Celestial Circle. Who could make such a wondrous morning as this but the Great King?

Adam Beam heard the *bump* against his bedroom door. He yawned and stretched and rolled happily over the side of his bed, feeling the carpet *skwish* between his toes while he walked to the bedroom door and swung it open.

"*Noooo…!*"

But it was too late! The huge paws of the great Siberian tiger hit Adam's chest, knocking him onto his back. The gigantic beast held Adam against the carpet and opened its powerful jaws.

"Noooo!" Adam yelled, staring into the red, open

mouth that bared three-inch fangs in rows of knife-sharp teeth.

"Noooo!" Adam turned his face to the side, and then started to giggle as the tiger's big, broad tongue licked Adam's face roughly. Adam threw his arm around the beautiful yellow, orange, and black-striped neck in a loving hug.

"Good morning, Toby!" Adam kissed the yellow thatch of hair on one side of the cat's face. Tiger fur tickled his face.

Adam jumped up from the floor and onto the cat's back.

"Hurry Toby! Let's eat!"

The huge cat loped down the hallway to the top of the stairway and half-slid and half-bumped his way to the bottom of the staircase so that Adam hardly jostled at all.

"Hello, boys." Bud Beam smiled brightly as Adam hopped to the kitchen floor. *"Catch, Toby!"* Mr. Beam tossed a red fruiton in the direction of the cat who chomped it happily and opened his mouth for more.

Bud Beam laughed. "Let's see. We might have another one here." He put his hand into the fruitonizer and brought out the rich red fruiton that had appeared as if by magic.

Toby stretched his huge yellow and black-striped body. His long, thick tail whipped and curled with anticipation. Bud Beam tossed the fruit. Toby caught it with ease in his wide jaws.

"Good boy!"

Toby stood ready to catch yet another fruiton.

"That's enough. Here, Adam, give him his catvage." Adam's dad ran his hand along the top of the manna manger, in which materialized a large portion of the golden brown tiger food.

Toby sniffed at his breakfast and followed it with his nose as Adam placed the meal upon the special eating table Mr. Beam had made for Adam's pet.

"I hear there are big things cooking at Explore-time," Mr. Beam said, rubbing Adam's dark brown hair on his way to pick up his briefcase that sat on the kitchen cabinet.

"Yes sir," Adam said. "We start Dream Doors today!"

"Dream Doors!" Mr. Beam said with excitement. "What a wonderful thing!"

"I can't wait! Did you ever go through a Dream Door?" Adam asked, running his hand atop the manna manger and pulling out the meal he chose for this morning's breakfast.

"No. Dream Doors are for New Eden children, and you know I was born in the Before Time."

"Oh, yeah…I forgot." Adam's thoughts caused a question to form. "Dad…why was the Before Time so different from now? Wasn't there anything fun to do?"

Adam's father lifted the briefcase from the counter and said, "Yes … there were some fun things to do, but that was before the Great Taking Away."

"Tell me again about the Great Taking Away," Adam said.

Mr. Beam put the briefcase on the floor and sat in a chair across from his son. His eyebrows narrowed in thought when he tried to remember those days long past.

"It's been so long, more than 107 years ago. But there are a few things that are fun to remember." Bud Beam leaned forward, placing his elbows on the table and rubbing his chin.

"Many years ago, in the Before Time, before the Great Taking Away and the Trouble Time, we would get in snowball fights while we waited for the school bus to pick us up. That was lots of fun."

Mr. Beam smiled, remembering the time he hit his best friend Joey with a snowball. Joey's shirt had filled with the icy powder when the snow exploded against his shoulder.

"What's a school bus?" Adam asked, twisting his nose and lips in an expression that said the term both amused him and made him curious.

"Where I grew up, a place called Brooklyn, New York, a school bus was just a way to get us to school. You remember I told you what a school was, don't you?"

Adam scrunched his nose again, his eyes turned up in concentration. "That was like Exploretime is for kids now."

"That's right. School was where we went to learn all kinds of things, but in the Before Time, kids couldn't go on Dreams Door Adventures. We had to sit at our desks and read books and our teachers would teach us about things. We couldn't actually go to the places in our minds. Our imaginations could not go from our heads then."

"Why not?"

"Because it was different then," Bud Beam said sadly. "The time before the return of the Great King...*everything* was different then." Adam's dad thought for a moment. "Although there were many good things about those days, there were many bad things that happened, too."

Mr. Beam fidgeted with his briefcase handle while he reflected further. "Then one day, everything changed in a flash. Millions of people vanished."

Adam straightened in his chair. "They just disappeared?" He'd heard about the Great Taking Away many times, but the amazing event always stirred his imagination.

"Yes, they just disappeared." Bud Beam's eyes brightening when a little girl ran past her brother and flung her arms around her father.

"How's my Sunbeam today?" he said, lifting his daughter into his lap and returning her hug.

Zonia kissed her dad's cheek and hugged his neck tightly again. "I get to go through a Dream Door!" Zonia said excitedly.

"Wonderful! You will have a terrific time!"

"Will you come with us?" Zonia questioned happily.

"Dream Doors are for children of the New Eden only. But I'll be with you in my thoughts."

Toby, lying near Mr. Beam's chair, stretched and gently bit the fuzzy cloth of one foot of Zonia's pajama bottom.

"Good morning, Toby!" Zonia said pulling the

foot of the pajamas from the tiger's teeth-clinched grip. She struggled from her father's lap and pounced on the big cat. Toby licked her face before she could pull away.

"New Eden is *indeed* a long way from Brooklyn, New York, and the Before Time," Bud Beam said in almost a whisper, watching his giggling little girl tussle with the 1,000-pound tiger.

Chapter 2

TOBY'S BIG YELLOW AND BLACK-STRIPED TAIL SWISHED and he paced back and forth while their mother gave Adam and Zonia instructions for the day. The tiger knew Adam and Zonia were about to leave in the Wind Way.

"You listen carefully to the teacher and the Lighton," Molly Beam said, straightening her daughter's shirt. She turned to Adam and smoothed down his hair. "It was so nice of you to invite your sister." She kissed him on the cheek. "This will be a great day!"

Toby crept closer and closer until Mrs. Beam noticed him. "Yes, Toby, you will have a fabulous day here with me too." She patted him on his broad head. He purred and pushed against her hand, trying to get her to scratch him behind his ears.

"Isn't Toby coming with us?" Zonia asked, hugging the cat.

"My Brighton said it's okay to bring pets," Adam said.

Molly Beam thought a second. "I had better make sure it's okay. Let me check." She shut her eyes and thought, *"To Adam's Dream Doors Brighton. May the children bring their pets to Exploretime today?"*

The answer came to Molly's mind instantly. *"Yes. Toby is welcome."*

"Looks like Toby can go too," Mrs. Beam said brightly, patting the tiger's head. Toby's long tail twitched happily in the air.

"It's time for the Wind Way. Have a good day at Exploretime and a great adventure in Dream Doors." Molly bent to kiss Adam and Zonia. See you both this evening…and you, too, Toby."

Adam, Zonia, and Toby disappeared with a swishing sound.

* * *

"GOOD MORNING, ADAM," Mrs. Levin, said when Adam, Zonia and Toby appeared in the Exploretime cube. "And this must be your sister, Zonia…and who is this?" Adam's Exploretime teacher patted Toby's big head and smiled.

"Toby," Adam said.

Toby shut his eyes and purred, fully enjoying the attention. "My, he's a beautiful tiger!" the teacher said, turning then to Zonia.

"I'm so glad you can join us for Dream Doors, Zonia." Mrs. Levin patted the little girl's cheek with her fingertips. "Dream Doors is the best learning time of all. You will be very glad you came!"

Zonia said, "I'm glad I came, too!"

Mrs. Levin guided the children to the small desks. "The other kids will be here in a moment."

Toby sat beside Adam as Mrs. Levin greet the other children who materialized out of thin air in the Exploretime cube.

Zonia was delighted by the parade of pets that accompanied Adam's Exploretime classmates.

Toby was delighted too. He snarled a low, happy snarl as pets small and large pop out of nothingness into the Exploretime cube. The Wind Way brought children, and pets of every size, color and type, in the twinkling of an eye from all over Glorainia to this marvelous place of adventure.

Once all the children had arrived, the cube filled with bright swirling colors. With a brilliant flash, a Lighton appeared. He stood more than eight feet tall and glowed in a dazzling golden-red and emerald-green light. Zonia had to squint as he smiled down at the children.

"I am Zekor, Lighton of your Exploretime Brighton," the Lighton said in a gentle voice that nonetheless echoed throughout the Exploretime cube. "Are you ready for your Dream Doors adventure?"

"*YES!*" The children screamed happily, barely able to stay seated behind their desks. Toby's tail swished back and forth, his yellow eyes fixed on the Lighton, who towered almost to the ceiling.

Zekor said, "Each of you and the one you have

chosen to go with you will enter your Dream Door in a moment." The Lighton stretched out his long, powerful arm. A burst of light sparked from the end of his fingertips. There appeared something that glowed almost as brightly as the Lighton. "But first, you must learn about dream drawing."

He held a belt-like glowing object with his shining fingertips, showing it to the children. "This is the dream doodler, and you must wear it at all times during your Dream Doors Adventure," he said with great excitement in his voice. "The dream doodler will take you everywhere you want to go within your Dream Door Adventure."

The children's eyes followed the shining hand as it took a curious device from the dream doodle belt. "First let me show you how it works." Zekor waved the Dream Doodler in the air leaving a tail of shimmering light with each stroke. A scene with a green forest and snow-topped mountains appeared suspended in mid-air in front of the children. Their mouths and eyes were wide with wonder.

Zekor said, "This is a Dream Door; a portal to amazing adventures!" He pointed to the children sitting at their desks. "And you will create these adventures yourselves."

The kids gasped. Some giggled. Some clapped their hands.

Zekor said, "When you go through your Dream Door, you enter your imagination." He ducked his head and shoulders and stepped into the picture. His bright, shimmering form quickly got smaller and smaller until it became no more than a pinpoint of light and disappeared. In the next second, the pinpoint of light appeared again, growing bigger and bigger until Zekor stepped back through the portal into the Exploretime cube. "And when your adventure is finished, you come back through the door."

Zekor's form glowed brighter. Sparkles of light twinkled and popped into the air. "Whatever you imagine, the dream doodler will draw into the air around you. When you step inside your dream-doodled scene you become part of the Dream Door vision you have created!"

The children *ooohed* and *aaahed*, pleased beyond measure with the Lighton's demonstration.

"Always remember who makes this possible for the children of New Eden."

"*PRAISE AND HONOR AND GLORY TO THE GREAT KING!*" the children shouted loudly as with one voice.

The Lighton smiled broadly and his approving laughter pulsed through the Exploretime cube. "To the Great King be honor and glory and praise and power indeed!"

Chapter 3

"Remember, now…" Mrs. Levin bent slightly to touch Adam's cheek and Zonia's straw-colored hair. "…Never take the responsibility of handling the dream doodler lightly. Only think the kind of thoughts the Great King wants you to think. Do you understand, Adam?"

"Yes, Mrs. Levin," Adam said, strapping the dream doodler belt around his waist and snapping its buckle shut.

"And you, Zonia, stay close to your brother, okay?"

"Yes, Mrs. Levin," Zonia said with just a bit of worry in her voice.

"Now, don't be afraid. There is nothing more fun than Dream Doors, as you will see." The teacher hugged both children.

Adam said, "Where will our Dream Door take us today?"

"The Bible time Before the Flood has been chosen for your first Dream Doors Adventure."

"*Quantum!*" Adam said excitedly. "That's my favorite Bible time!"

Mrs. Levin chuckled, remembering that in her day, in the Before Time, the expression had been, "*Cool!*"

"*Quantum!*" Zonia said, trying to match her brother's enthusiasm.

The teacher was glad to see that excitement had replaced the little girl's nervousness.

Toby growled playfully, twitching his tail with anticipation. The teacher urged the children to the center of the Exploretime cube.

"Just use your imagination, Adam," Mrs. Levin said. "Imagine you're in the world before the Flood, and then push the green "DREAM DRAW" button on your dream doodler and wave the dream doodler in the air."

Adam pulled the dream doodler from its holster. It was heavy, and shaped like a big purple flashlight, with a cone on the front of it, shaped like a long, tapered pearl. It had three buttons: A green button surrounded with the words, *Dream Draw*. A red button with the word *Out*. And a blue button labeled *Disappear Dazzler*.

He shut his eyes, and thought of First Time world, remembering it from pictures he'd seen in a book of stories from that time. He thought of tall trees and green ferns, and pterodactyls.

Adam pushed the green "DREAM DRAW"

button and quickly waved the dream doodler. He opened his eyes. The picture that had been inside his head hung in the air in front of them.

"It's a beautiful Dream Door!" Mrs. Levin said. "Don't you think so, Zonia?"

"*Quantum!*" Adam's sister said quietly, though with enthusiasm.

Toby's tail gave a few extra twitches. He turned his head curiously when the teacher said, "Now don't be afraid. You can come out of your Dream Door Adventure simply by pushing the red 'OUT' button."

Adam took Zonia's hand and she held tightly to the fur on Toby's neck.

"Remember, the Lightons are watching," Mrs. Levin said

Adam, Zonia, and Toby stepped through the Dream Door portal. A sudden wind drew them through it. Before them swirled a beautiful array of lights. The whirling became faster and faster and Adam felt his feet lift from the floor while the twisting wind drew them ever deeper into the tunnel-like whirlpool.

"*Ooohhh!*" Zonia exclaimed, holding tightly to a tuft of Toby's fur. The tiger snarled a surprised snarl. Adam could only say, "*Quantum!*"

* * *

A FEW SECONDS LATER ADAM, Zonia and Toby gently settled their feet and paws onto the solid ground.

The wind had stopped twirling. Adam and Zonia looked all about them. They were in a lush forest. Several large creatures sailed high above and between the trees.

"Where are we, Adam?" Zonia asked after several seconds of wonderment.

"I don't know, but look at the size of those trees!"

The trees were huge, far taller than any he had seen. Taller than even the giant redwoods of New Eden.

"We must be in the Before Time, in the time Before the Flood," Adam said.

Toby growled his opinion, looking up at the large bird-like creatures gliding in silent circles high above the forest.

"Look! Pterodactyls!" Adam said, pointing in the direction of the flying beasts.

"But they are extinct," Zonia said.

"They weren't extinct in the time Before the Flood."

A loud scream from above and behind them pierced the air. Startled, they turned to see a gigantic pterodactyl diving toward them. The flying creature swept across them, barely missing them with a *swoosh* and a strong rush of wind.

Toby snarled and stood over the children, his paws flailing in the air at the raptor when it again passed over.

"*Use the dream doodler, Adam,*" Zekor's voice said calmly inside Adam's head. "*Think about a safer place.*"

"Here it comes again!" Zonia cried.

Toby prepared to defend against the attack. The reptile flew straight at them, its mouth wide, showing jagged rows of teeth, its snake-like tail whipping behind its talons.

Toby leaped and knocked the bird aside with one sweeping blow of his big paw. The pterodactyl screamed angrily and swept upward in order to prepare for another attack.

Adam held out the dream doodler and thought of a safer place. A place with pleasant flower smells. A place with no pterodactyls. He pushed the green button and waved the dream doodler in the air.

With a whoosh, the air split apart. They could see through the opening, the scene of open sky and landscape decorated with beautiful flowers. A small winding brook gurgled peacefully.

"Quick! Through the opening!" Adam ordered, and the three of them sprang through the portal and into the magnificent dream drawing.

"*Quantum!*" Adam said with amazement.

"*YES!*" Zonia added, equally amazed.

Toby surveyed their surroundings and snarled a curious though pleased snarl.

"Wh…Where are we, Adam?" Zonia asked quietly.

"I don't know" her brother said almost as quietly while his eyes, wide with wonder, scanned the scene. Zonia clutched Toby's fur and stood as close to the tiger as possible. The three of them walked slowly, each seeing the brightly colored flowers of every description which grew to heights far above them. The flowers were more like trees than flowers. Their stems were as big around as his legs, and the leaves were big enough to make a shirt or a pair of trousers or a blanket!

Flowers covered the land as far as they could see, but the huge trees were no longer in view. Adam, Zonia and Toby walked for what seemed like hours to Adam's sister. "I'm getting hungry," she said rather mournfully. "And tired."

Toby growled a low growl of complaint.

Adam took the dream doodler from its holster and examined the instrument. "Neither Mrs. Levin nor the Zekor had said anything about food. But we can always punch the red "OUT" button."

"And I'm thirsty," Zonia moaned. She sat on a large flat-topped stone.

Adam continued to study the dream doodler. "*Hmmh*. I wonder…" he said quietly.

"You wonder…*what*?" Zonia asked while lying back on the stone to rest. Toby sat beside her and gave her a big wet lick on her cheek.

"Ew." She sat up, wiping the wetness away with the sleeve of her shirt.

"There's no water around here, that's for sure," Adam said. "Let's try this."

He waved the dream doodler while pressing on the green "DREAM DRAW" button, his eyes closed in concentration. An opening suddenly appeared out of nothingness, another beautiful scene hanging in midair.

Adam said, "Hurry, Zonia…Toby! Jump through the opening!"

The three of them leaped through the portal and found themselves surrounded by even thicker and more lush plant life than before. They heard the sound of gurgling water. Adam searched for but couldn't find the source of the sound. "It's got to be here somewhere," he said, bending to look beneath the branches of leaves and flowers. Toby squatted low and slipped through an opening in the bushes.

"The water must be this way!" Adam said, taking Zonia's hand and leading her through the bushes where Toby had entered. In a moment they found the cat at the edge of a small stream lapping water. They joined him, leaning on their hands and knees, bending to sip the cold, refreshing water.

"This water…*quantum*!" Zonia said, wiping her face and mouth with her sleeve after having drunk her fill.

"*Listen*!" Adam said in a hushed tone.

"What is it?"

"*Ssshh*." Adam looked up stream. A rumbling sound was growing louder and louder.

"What is that sound?!" Zonia said.

Suddenly, a wall of water was rushing toward them.

Toby understood the danger and nudged the children together. They climbed onto his back. Adam wrapped his arms tightly around the tiger's neck. Zonia held onto Adam's waist. The next moment the water swept them downstream.

Even Toby could not control the rolling, tumbling tide. Any moment the three of them would be separated!

Zonia shouted, "Dream Door us out of here!"

Of course! He'd forgotten about the Dream Doodler. It had saved them from the pterodactyl, it could do the same now.

With one arm still around the tiger's neck, Adam fumbled with the dream doodler, finally managing to pull it from its holster. A roaring sound grew louder while the water gushed at them ever faster. A waterfall!

Almost too late! Adam closed his eyes just as they reached the waterfall's edge. He pushed the "DREAM DRAW" button and waved the dream doodler in the direction of the waterfall.

Adam, Zonia, and Toby shot through a Dream Door opening that had appeared at the waterfall's edge. Each of them did somersaults, finally coming to a stop in a thick thatch of gigantic clover leaves.

Toby was the first to regain his balance. He nudged the children with his nose and licked them with his tongue, making sure they were not hurt.

"Boy, that was a close one!" Adam said, getting to his feet and helping his sister to hers.

"Look! We're not even wet!" Zonia said, patting her brother's shirt and then her own clothing.

"*Quantum*!" Adam said. He brushed the leaves from the dream doodler, and smiled at the amazing device.

* * *

THE VALLEY below reflected the bright golden sky above.

Adam, Zonia and Toby carefully made their way down the steep slope, their sliding feet causing stones to tumble in front of them. Just ahead, a gigantic boulder stood in their path. They would have to circle around and through an opening that only one at a time could pass through.

Adam was the first to start through the opening, ducking his head to avoid the boulder's overhang. Zonia was close behind, followed by Toby, who sensed something was not right. The tiger gently seized the little girl by the seat of her pants and tugged her backwards.

"Toby, *let go*! What are you doing?"

It was too late for Adam, who was already into the opening. A huge, slithering, gray wall of some sort fell over the opening, blocking his way. Toby held Zonia down with one huge paw and grabbed Adam by the pants leg with the other paw, and dragged him back to where his sister lay.

The tiger growled loudly and reared on his back feet. Zonia screamed when she saw the giant snake's head above the boulder. Its mouth was wide open and its forked tongue flickered in the air toward them.

"Adam! A giant snake!" she said, pointing for her brother to look up at the sky above the boulder.

The snake was twice as big around as Toby, its yellow, slitted eyes glaring at them above, it's the sharp fangs at least two feet long. The children, never afraid of snakes because snakes were harmless in New Eden, nonetheless stood unable to move, terrified at this creature. They had never seen a snake this large. Adam remembered stories about snakes in the Before Time and the Trouble Time. They were deadly back then, but he had never heard stories about them being as big as this one. This was not the Before Time or the Trouble Time, but the time Before the Flood! They must get away from this snake!

The reptile lowered its head and upper part of its body onto the stone and started slithering toward them, continuing to flicker its wicked tongue in their direction.

Toby swiped at the serpent and moved to get between it and the children.

All three of them backed up. Adam removed the dream doodler from its holster.

I must think of the valley below, he thought. "I want us to be safely in the valley below!"

He pushed the green button and waved the dream doodler. The space between the kids and the snake split apart in midair and the three ran through the opening. In the next instant, they stood beneath overhanging tree limbs, each limb sagging because of the varieties of fruit that hung from them.

Thoughts of the huge snake made Zonia shiver and she trembled while her brother held her tightly.

"It's okay, Zonia. The Dream Doodler saved us again."

Toby seemed to understand Adam's words. The

tiger nuzzled his face against Zonia's, and softly growled a purring growl, his whiskers as thick as pencils tickling her skin. He seemed to want to add to Adam's comforting words.

Toby stretched his great body as far as he could stretch, and with one mighty swipe of a huge paw, brought a number of the luscious-looking fruit from one branch.

They sat in picnic fashion near the trunk of one of the big trees and ate their fill before getting to their feet.

Zonia said, "What do we do now? Where are we going?"

Toby cocked his head curiously and looked at Adam.

"There's a path there, through those woods. Let's see where it leads." Adam's confident words set the three of them walking down the small, almost grass-less path that narrowed in the distance, then disappeared into the forest.

"It sure is dark," Zonia said, looking around and above at the thick foliage.

The children of Glorainia rarely knew darkness because all was bright and golden and pure. Zonia more and more thought about home the further into the forest they went.

Soon they came into an opening where a pool of hot water bubbled. Clouds of steam shot into the air every few seconds and made hissing noises. The dark trunks of the trees surrounded the pool in an almost perfect circle. Flat stones lay around the pool, Adam noticed, as if arranged as places to sit.

Thin streams of light from above shone between the tree tops.

Zonia thought, *it is a little brighter here, although it is very spooky.*

Suddenly, the rays of light seemed to become clouded over and the hissing sounds got louder.

Toby sensed something was not right and moved in front of the children, blocking their way from going nearer the pool. Adam and Zonia put their hands upon the tiger's neck. The opening grew darker and darker. Adam felt for the dream doodler at his side. He felt comfort in knowing that it was still there.

The darkness grew denser. Now they could barely see the bubbling pool, or each other, for that matter.

In the next moment, glowing yellow eyes – many, many eyes – blinked and peered at them from the dark woods that surrounded the opening. The glowing yellow eyes began moving closer and closer.

Adam, Zonia and Toby backed up nearer to the center of the opening until they stood at the edge of the hot, gurgling pool.

Figures that had arms but that did not seem to have legs appeared to float from the dark forest surrounding them. The figures wore dark, hooded robes of purple or black. Adam couldn't tell exactly which. The only light seemed to come from the eyes that blinked within the hoods of the floating shapes that now surrounded them and the pool.

Adam took out the dream doodler and held it tight. The figures came ever closer.

Toby snarled an angry snarl and started toward the figures, causing them to stop their advance.

"*Toby!*" Adam shouted.

The tiger stopped, baring his three-inch-long fangs at the shapes. One of the robed figures moved forward. A scratchy, echoing voice came from within its dark hood. "Why are you here? What is your purpose? Who sent you?"

Adam, clutching the dream doodler tightly in his right hand, spoke timidly at first, then in a louder voice. "We came through a Dream Door. I don't know why we are here. It's part of Exploretime."

Toby crouched to attack the threatening creature.

"*Toby! No!*" Adam commanded. The tiger relaxed from its crouched position.

The figure grew larger. Its voice became angry and the yellow eyes grew more menacing. "You are wise, young one," the echoing voice said from within the hood. "The three of you would make a very fine meal."

Adam's finger moved to the "DREAM DRAW" button on the dream doodler. He held his sister tightly with his left arm around her and the two of them backed even closer to the pool of boiling water.

"It's the apples! It's the apples, isn't it?" the creature screeched.

For the first time, Adam and Zonia could see the sharp, jagged teeth beneath the glowing yellow eyes within the darkness of the hood.

"*HE* has sent you to find the apples! Well, you will proceed no further." The voice calmed and ended with a wicked chuckle. Long, white, bony fingers emerged from the sleeves of the robe and waved angrily. "We shall have you all for dinner!" the creature said, moving slowly forward.

Adam, Zonia, and Toby backed up to the edge of the pool of bubbling, scalding water.

Chapter 4

"*Nothing can hurt you in Dream Doors.*"

Adam heard Zekor's words clearly in his mind and he found courage in them. His eyes narrowed in determination and his finger moved toward the green Dream Draw button.

Zonia was not so sure. She had not heard the voice. She held tightly to the thick fur on Toby's neck. The tiger moved to put himself between the children and the floating hooded figures with their robed arms outstretched eerily, their bony white fingers reaching, grabbing.

"*The apples are important, very important,*" the Lighton's voice said again in Adam's mind. "*You must think of the apples…seven apples … before you push the 'DREAM DRAW' button!*"

The groaning, hooded beings almost touched them. Now, Adam and Zonia could see their ghostly skull-like faces with within the dark hoods. Sharp white teeth gnashing to get at them.

Adam thought about seven apples and shut his eyes. He pressed the green button, waving the dream doodler in the air. A dark scene opened up before his.

"Quick! Into the dream drawing!" Adam shouted, pulling his sister by her arm as he charged through the opening that had appeared in midair.

Toby led the way, powerfully tugging Adam, who held Toby's long, thick tail with one hand and his sister's arm with the other.

Their new surroundings, when they had passed through the dream drawing portal, were dark. Very dark. Only the tiger could see well enough to avoid bumping into the rocky sides of the dark place.

"Stay close." Adam said. He need not have worried. Zonia clutched him so tightly she nearly squeezed the breath from him.

"Where are we now?" Zonia asked with trembling in her voice.

"It's a cave, I think," Adam answered. "I sure wish we had a light."

The dream doodler! Of course. Adam pushed the green button, and waved the instrument.

A small opening appeared brightly in the darkness of the cave and Adam reached his hand through the portal.

"A light!" he said happily as he withdrew a large flashlight.

Toby watched curiously as Adam turned on the powerful beam and moved it over the walls and floor of the cave. "Come on. Let's see where this leads, and don't worry, I'll draw us out of this place if I have to," Adam said with the confidence of an experienced Dream Door explorer.

The three made their way slowly and carefully further into the cave. The big shaft of light lit up the shadowy, jagged sides and the rocky floor while they walked along the twisting, turning pathway.

After a few minutes of winding their way through the small tunnel, they stepped into a big cavern. When the flashlight beam hit the ceiling of the cavern, the whole room filled with thunderous flapping sights and sounds. Zonia grabbed Adam, nearly knocking the flashlight from his hands.

"It's just bats," Adam said, trying to make his sister and himself feel less frightened.

Toby snarled, his head jerking back and forth as he watched the hundreds of bats flap their way out of the cavern until all was quiet again.

Adam and his sister had never known about being afraid. Adam remembered reading and hearing stories about children in the Trouble Time and the Before Time and the many things there were that might harm them. But he and Zonia and the other children of New Eden time had no need to fear anything. The Brightons had often told the children that the Great King had changed everything for the better since the Trouble Time and the Before Time.

Dream Doors, the Brightons had told Adam and the other children, were for learning about other places and other times...ancient times...and what things were like for the children of those days. There was no reason to be afraid, ever, the Brightons always had assured them. The Great King would never allow harm to come to the children of New Eden time. Dream Doors were sometimes a bit scary perhaps—but never dangerous.

But it felt dangerous now!

The words of the Brightons reassured Adam. "The Great King will protect us always, Zonia. Our Lighton is with us."

Zonia relaxed her grip on his arm, but squeezed Toby's fur just a bit tighter with her other hand. Zonia had not had the Dream Door Adventures talk from the Brightons yet, but she trusted her brother who led the way, shining the light in the direction he thought the bats had left the cavern.

"There must be a way out," Adam said, walking toward a small tunnel where the bats had flown through. Adam went in first, followed by Zonia, then Toby. Soon the tunnel narrowed till it was barely big enough for the big cat to crawl through on his stomach. Finally, they came out on the other side of the narrow crawlway into another cavern. This one was much smaller than the one with the bats.

"Look! Up there!" Adam pointed the light at the ceiling of the cavern. "There's the opening that the bats flew through."

"How will we be able to get up to that hole? It's really high," Zonia said, looking around the tall, walled cavern. "There isn't any place else to go... there aren't any more tunnels we can go through."

Adam again shined the flashlight around the walls of the cavern. Zonia was right; there was only one way out, and that was up through the roof of the cave.

He *could* push the "DREAM DRAW" button and create another dream drawing through which they could escape. Something in the back of his mind told him to explore this hole in the roof. If he drew another portal drawing for them, he was not sure where it would lead. He *must* try to get out through the hole in the roof.

Adam thought about the problem and suddenly he knew what they needed.

"A ladder!" Adam said with enthusiasm. "That's what we need, a ladder!"

"Where are we going to get a ladder?" Zonia said with just a bit of irritation in her voice.

Adam said, "Let's see if this will work." He took the dream doodler from its holster. He shut his eyes and pointed it at the hole in the roof of the cavern. He made several strokes up and down with the dream doodler, then opened his eyes.

"Look! It's a ladder!" Zonia said happily. "A ladder going all the way from the bottom to the top… but what about Toby?"

Zonia was right again. The heavy tiger would never be able to climb the ladder. Not a ladder that was straight up and down like this one. "I'll fix that!" Adam said, shutting his eyes and pointing the dream doodler again at the opening in the ceiling. After several more strokes up and down, the ladder changed form. It became a stairway with wide steps that led from the floor of the cavern to one side of the hole.

Zonia clapped her hands and giggled approval. "*Quantum!*" she said, hugging Toby. "Now you can climb out with us." Toby looked at the staircase, which had changed from its previous form as a ladder and snarled a snarl of approval.

"Of course, I could've dream doodled him and us through that hole if I had wanted to," Adam said, talking to himself more than to Zonia.

When the children and the tiger had crawled through the opening and onto the top of the gigantic boulder that was the roof of the cave, they looked back into the hole they had just left. They watched the staircase vanish.

Suddenly, sounds from behind them startled them. They heard voices of many children talking excitedly in hushed tones, then becoming quiet.

Adam, Zonia and Toby stood staring at the group of children, who stood staring back at them. The children backed away from Adam, his sister and their tiger, their eyes wide with fear.

Adam and Zonia had never seen children wearing clothing like this. Instead of pants, shirts and shoes, they wore cloth that covered them from shoulders to feet. But they were children just like them; that was easy enough to see.

"Why are you afraid? Don't be afraid of us," Adam said in a friendly voice. "We won't hurt you."

Toby snarled a friendly snarl. The children's eyes

and mouths widened with fear, and they began running in all directions.

Toby cocked his head curiously, his long tail twitching. The tiger looked at Adam.

"I don't know what's wrong with them," Adam said to the cat, who seemed to want to know why the children scattered in all directions.

Chapter 5

THEY MADE THEIR WAY DOWN FROM THE BIG, ROUND boulder that covered the cave. The other children were nowhere in sight.

"I wonder where they went?" Zonia asked, standing with her hands on her hips, looking all around at the rocks, the high grass, the bushes and trees. "Why are they afraid of us?"

"I think it's Toby...they are afraid of Toby," Adam said.

The tiger snarled a curious snarl and cocked his head, looking at Adam.

Zonia cocked her head, as had Toby. "Why should they be afraid of Toby?"

"Don't you see? We're in the First Time. In the times before New Eden, tigers, lions, and many of the animals were dangerous. Remember Mom and Dad telling us about that? Those kids think Toby is dangerous!"

Toby snarled a snarl of disapproval, then stood with his long tail swishing disapproving swishes.

"Toby wouldn't hurt anyone!" Zonia said with disbelief in her voice.

Adam said, "You know that and I know that, but they don't know that."

Adam was thinking of ways to bring the children out of hiding.

So was Zonia. "I know!" she said excitedly. "Let's pet Toby and then they will know he doesn't hurt kids!"

That sounded like a good idea to Adam, who, like his sister, began petting Toby, then nuzzling his face against the tiger's.

Toby didn't know what the sudden affection was all about, but he quickly returned their love with licks of his wide, wet tongue. Adam and Zonia wiped their faces with their shirtsleeves, giggling and trying to get away from the big tongue's lapping.

Adam grabbed the tiger around the neck and hopped up on Toby's back. Zonia continued hugging and kissing the yellow and black-striped face.

"See!" Adam said, shouting while sitting astride the huge tiger's back. "Toby won't hurt you!"

Children of Glorainia and of all New Eden could understand each other perfectly. It was not so much that there were no different languages, it was simply that the Great King had given the children of the Kingdom the ability to overcome all language barriers. And so children of this ancient time...the First Time...talked freely. But more than that, they understood the language of love being spoken between the gigantic cat and his two human friends.

The bravest of the group, a boy who looked to be about Adam's age, came shyly out of the bushes.

The other children came one by one from the hedges. They stood behind the first boy who had come into the opening.

"Hello. What's your name?" Adam asked the apparent leader of the group. "My name is Adam," he quickly added.

The boy stood quietly, letting his eyes meet Adam's briefly before glancing down at the ground, then back at Adam. "Enoch," he answered in just above a whisper.

"Hello, Enoch," Adam said boldly. "This is my sister, Zonia."

Zonia smiled shyly, standing somewhat behind her brother, who had just hopped off Toby's back.

All the children eyed the tiger suspiciously, their eyes filled with amazement that the beast and the two strangers seemed to be as friendly with each other as they themselves were with their own pets.

"Don't be afraid of Toby," Adam said. "He loves kids."

The dark-haired boy said with a little more confidence in his voice, "I just hope he doesn't love to EAT kids." Enoch's expression said that he was only half joking.

Adam and Zonia laughed and said, "He doesn't eat kids. The only thing he likes...*really* likes...are fruitons." Toby growled a purring growl of agreement.

Enoch looked warily at the tiger, and then said, "What are fruitons?"

"Oh…they are types of food, kind of like fruit, you know, peaches, pears plums, that sort of thing. Only they are especially made for tigers."

Enoch's face again showed an expression of amazement. Who were these strange kids who had the biggest tiger he had ever seen for a playmate? Kids who dressed oddly and came from a place where tigers ate fruit prepared especially for them?

The other children spread out at Enoch's side so they could get a better look at the two strange kids and the tiger.

"Do you live in the cave hole?" Enoch asked.

"The cave hole?" Adam at first did not understand, but then realized that it must have looked to these kids as if he, Zonia and Toby actually lived in the cave from which they suddenly appeared.

"No. We don't live in that cave. We were lost."

The children mumbled quietly to each other, their eyes wide with amazement.

"What's wrong?" Adam said, seeing their astonishment.

Enoch said, "It is the place of the slegna. Human children never go into the cave hole. Only muton children."

"Slegna? Mutons? Who are they, and why can't kids go in there?" Adam was truly puzzled. There was no place in New Eden children were not allowed.

Enoch seemed to become less trusting. He and the other children seemed puzzled that Adam and Zonia did not know about the slegna and the mutons. They mumbled again among themselves and looked suspiciously at Adam and his sister.

Adam said, "We did see some really weird guys. They wore black robes and floated in the air and had long, white, bony-looking fingers. But that was before we went through the Dream Door and ended up in that cave." Adam spoke with no hint of fear in his voice. That, too, caused mumbling among the other children.

"Slegna! ...Those were slegna," Enoch said just above a whisper.

Enoch thought. *How could two children, even with the help of the biggest tiger he had ever seen...meet up with the slegna in the regions below, yet somehow come through safely? No one who went into the cave of the hole ever came out again!*

"I guess you already know it, but we aren't from around here," Adam said, interrupting Enoch's thoughts. "It's hard to explain. We are from another place. Another time."

Enoch and his companions no longer mumbled among themselves, but just stared at the three strangers.

Adam broke the uncomfortable silence after a few seconds. "You don't have to be afraid of us. We're just kids like you."

Enoch thought they looked like kids. But they definitely were not like he and his friends. There were no tigers for pets among them. Tigers ate children, not peaches, pears, apples and plums.

"Look. I'll prove it to you. We came here by using this." Adam pulled the dream doodler from its holster and held it out for Enoch and the others to see. "I can draw a picture with this and then step into the picture. That's how we got here. That's how we came to your time. This is only a Dream Door Adventure as part of Exploretime."

The children obviously didn't make any sense of what Adam had said.

"Okay. I'll prove it to you. I will dream draw a place. Then we can all go there together."

Adam pushed the "DREAM DRAW" button and waved the dream doodler in the air, closing his eyes and thinking about a place all the children might enjoy. A Dream Door suddenly appeared in mid-air and beyond the portal a magnificent landscape with a high mountain whose peak was covered with snow. Below it were tall, green trees and beautiful flowers of many colors.

"See? I can walk right into it and stay there as long as I like." Adam looked from the Dream Door portal back to the direction of the children, they had all disappeared again. "Where did they go?"

"I think you scared them," Zonia said.

Toby was staring at the bushes, his long tail twitching in the air.

* * *

ADAM AND ZONIA searched for the children but not even Toby seemed to know the direction in which they had gone. It was as if they had left not even a scent for the tiger's sensitive nose and the thick grass was not good for making footprints.

"When will we have to be back at the Exploretime cube?" Zonia asked, growing tired of looking for the kids and beginning to miss her mom. "Haven't we been gone a really long time?"

"No, Zonia. The Lightons said that the time we spend in Dream Doors is not like time in New Eden. When we get back it will be almost the same time as when we left."

"No matter how long we stay here?"

"That's right. No matter how long we stay here."

Adam tried to sound confident, but he was kind of beginning to miss his mother and dad, too. "All I have to do is push the 'OUT' button and we will be right back in the Exploretime cube."

Adam spoke in a tone that pleaded for Zonia's understanding. "This is the time Before the Great Flood, Zonia. It's one of my favorite Bible Times. Let's look around for a while. I promise I'll use the dream doodler to take us home before long."

Zonia said in an impatient, sisterly way. "Okay. Can we find those kids with the dream doodler?"

"Of course!" Adam hadn't thought of that. He took the doodler from its holster, shut his eyes tightly, and thought of Enoch and the other children. He waved the instrument and the dream drawing split the very air. There they were! The kids! Many, many more of them than before!

Their backs were turned to Adam, Zonia and Toby, who watched them in the dream drawing. The children were gathered around something, but it was impossible to tell what. The kids seemed to be listening very carefully to someone they could not see from where they stood just inside the Dream Door.

"Let's go through very slowly and quietly," Adam said. "We don't want to scare them again."

"Isn't there a button or something on that thing that can make you disappear?" Zonia asked, remembering something the Lighton had told them.

"*Yeah!*" Adam looked at the dream doodler, finding a blue colored button at the bottom of its handle. "I forgot about this!"

Surrounding the small button were the words "DISAPPEAR DAZZLER."

"The Lightons said that anybody who touches the doodler when the 'DISAPPEAR' button is pushed will become invisible."

Zonia said excitedly. "But the ones who disappear can see each other, remember?"

"And when you push the button again, you become visible again." Adam grabbed his sister's hand and put it on the dream doodler. Together they placed it on the back of Toby's neck. The tiger's ears wiggled curiously and he snarled a gentle snarl.

Adam pressed the button. "That should do it," he said. "Quick! Into the dream drawing!"

When they ran through the dream drawing, the

portal closed behind them and like Adam, Zonia and Toby became invisible, yet they could still see each other.

"Let's get closer to them," Adam said, starting to walk toward the children.

"*Quiet, Toby…*" he said to the tiger, who gave Adam a curious look.

The three moved closer to the children crowded around an old man who sat on a rock. "Ssshh…they can't see us but they can still hear us," Adam whispered.

They stopped several feet away, afraid the children and the old man might hear their shuffling footsteps.

"It was a time when your grandmother and I had the whole Garden to ourselves," the old man was saying to the children, who sat on the ground in front of him. Other children draped their arms over his shoulders.

The smallest of the children leaned against his leg or nuzzled against his sides while he held them with his arms around them.

"It was a wonderful time. Grandmother Eve and I walked every evening in the cool mist with Him."

The old man had a pleasant smile on his face while he talked. Yet there was a faraway look in his eye, a faraway look that twinkled with remembrance. The children moved closer, each trying to get a better position than the others in order to hear their grandfather retell the story he had told so often. They never tired of hearing it.

Adam and Zonia could see by the age lines in the

man's face and around his eyes that he was very old indeed. His white hair had a certain shine about it, almost a glow that made it look as if there were a light shining directly on it from above. Although he was very old, he was very handsome, Zonia thought, and wished he were her grandfather, too.

"He loved us," the grandfather was saying, "… and made the whole Garden just for us to enjoy."

"What about the animals, Grandpa?" one of the older children asked. The others chimed in, "Yes! Tell us about the animals again!"

The old man smiled and squeezed the little ones closest to him, looking down at them.

"Ah, the animals. Always you want to hear about the animals." He laughed a hearty laugh, the twinkle in his eyes sparkling with his love for his many great, great, great, great grandchildren. "Okay then…the animals it is!"

Somehow Adam and Zonia were drawn to the old man as if they, too, were his grandchildren. Even Toby seemed to sense that this grandfather was somehow a very special grandfather.

"The first time I saw the animals, my eyes nearly popped out. All sorts of animals of nearly every kind," the old man said, his eyes wide while he looked into the equally wide eyes of all his grandchildren, who were taking in every word.

"He brought me the animals one by one. It took quite a long time, I can tell you," the grandfather said with a laugh. "But it was *so* much fun!"

Then, almost in a whisper, he added, "And you know what?"

The children grew very quiet, their eyes even wider with wonder.

"He wanted me to name each and every animal!"

"Even the elephant?" the youngest of the grandsons asked in astonishment.

"Even the elephant! The name fits him, doesn't it?"

The little grandson nodded his head *yes*.

"Even the tiger?" the youngest granddaughter asked, twisting her nose and mouth in an expression of amazement.

"*Especially* the tiger!" the grandfather said thoughtfully. The tiger was among the grandest of all."

Adam looked at Toby, who cocked his head and snarled a quiet snarl. Zonia hugged Toby's neck while keeping her eyes on the grandfather, whose storytelling was the best she had ever heard.

"They were all lovely…so very lovely," he said, his eyes again taking on that faraway look.

"And you mean you could walk right up to them?" another grandson asked with astonishment.

"Oh, yes. I could play with a full-grown tiger just the way you could play with a little kitten today," the grandfather said with a remembering smile.

"What happened, Grandfather? Why can't *we* play with the tigers like that?" one of the little granddaughters, who was holding a kitten asked longingly.

"Because in that day, we walked with Him. That was before…"

The old man looked downward. Adam and Zonia saw a single tear trickle from the corner of one eye.

One of the older grandsons—one who had heard the story many times—said, "It was before you and Grandmother did something you shouldn't. Isn't that right?".

The grandfather looked at his grandson who had asked the question and nodded his head *yes*.

"And He and you and Grandmother could no longer walk together in the Garden?"

"That's right, my son. The reason we cannot walk at peace with the animals was…*is*…my fault."

The grandfather dried his eyes with the sleeve of his robe. "But that was then, and this is now. He has forgiven and now we must live our lives as He wants us to."

Looking directly into the eyes of all his grandchildren, he said in a firmer, stronger voice, "One day, everyone will be able to again walk and play with the tiger. He will make things right again. He has promised. He cannot lie."

"*Grandfather!*"

"Yes, Enoch?" the grandfather said looking at the oldest great grandchild.

"We saw a boy and a girl today. They had a huge tiger with them. One of them jumped on its back."

All the grandchildren turned to look at Enoch.

"That's right, Grandfather!" Enoch's sister said. "I saw them, too. They were *strange* children, dressed in an odd way and I've never seen a tiger so big."

The old man's eyes brightened. "Come here,

Enoch." Enoch's grandfather pulled the boy close to him and held him with both hands-on Enoch's shoulders.

"You say the tiger was tame? You really saw these children? This is not a childish prank?"

"No, Grandfather! We really saw them!"

"Then what happened?" The grandfather stared earnestly into Enoch's eyes.

"At first we were afraid of the tiger. But it was a nice tiger, and stayed with those strange children, and then we were not quite so afraid."

"Yes, yes? What happened then?"

"They had this strange thing. The boy was wearing this thing around him. With it he…" Enoch hesitated, not sure how to describe what he saw.

"With it he what?" Enoch's grandfather was growing anxious to hear.

"He…he drew a picture in the air."

The old man took his hands off of his grandson's shoulders and sat back on the rock and looked at Enoch's sister. "Come closer, Telah," he said, reaching out his hand to her. "And did you see this strange boy draw a picture in the air?"

"Yes, Grandfather," Telah said. "It was a picture you could walk right into!"

"*Walk* into?" her grandfather looked at the other children. "You all saw this picture in the air, a picture you could walk right into?"

The children all nodded.

Strange children dressed in an odd manner…a huge tiger that did no harm to children…a picture drawn in mid-air…

could it be? The old man's thoughts came one after the other.

Long ago, the Creator of all things had told him about strangers who would come from a future time in which all things would be as they once were in the garden.

"Where did you see these children? I *must* talk to them," Enoch's grandfather said with great concern.

"We ran away and hid because we were afraid." Enoch was sorry to have to tell his grandfather this. He could see the disappointment in his face.

Adam Beam and his sister also saw the unhappiness Enoch's words had caused. Somehow, they both wished to make the old man feel better. Adam whispered, "I think it's time to show ourselves." His finger moved to the 'DISAPPEAR DAZZLER' button."

"It might scare them," Zonia said.

"I don't think so. They are with their grandfather and I don't think he is afraid of anything."

Chapter 6

Adam pressed the "DISAPPEAR DAZZLER" button and he and Zonia and Toby popped suddenly in full view of the children and their grandfather. The children gasped and hurried to surround the old man sitting on the rock, a startled look on his face.

"I'm sorry, sir," Adam said, somewhat shyly. "We didn't mean to frighten you."

The grandfather looked at first at the strangely dressed boy and girl, then at the gigantic tiger, who returned his stare with a curious cock of his black, yellow, orange and white-striped head.

The old man peered into the staring, yellow eyes of the cat. Toby gazed into the eyes of the old man, eyes that instantly filled with tears that spilled onto his cheeks.

"Toby?"

Toby came to the man and put his big paws on the man's shoulders. He gave him a big, wet lick.

The old man laughed. "Toby…a fabulous tiger indeed!" Enoch's grandfather stroked Toby's broad head with his hand.

Somehow, this old man knew, he *really* knew the tiger, even its name!

"From what strange land and what strange time do you come, tiger?" The man said, continuing to stroke Toby's head.

The grandchildren stood behind him, amazed that their grandfather had so easily won the friendship of this great beast. Not only that, but he knew the tiger's name as well.

Adam and Zonia were amazed. Zonia could contain her curiosity no longer. "How did you know Toby's name?" she blurted, asking the question all of the children wanted to know.

"It is a long story, little one. A *very* long story," the grandfather said, rising to his feet.

Toby rubbed against the man while growling a soft, purring growl.

Enoch worked up the courage to put his hand on Toby's back and pulled his hand quickly away. "He won't hurt you," Enoch's grandfather said. "Will you, boy?"

The old man smiled at the huge cat, who shut his eyes and growled a purring growl when the grandfather rubbed him behind one of his ears.

Enoch, trusting his grandfather, began stroking the cat, who turned around and gave him a big lick in the face. Like children always did when Toby licked them, Enoch giggled and wiped his face with the back of his hand. "Why is this tiger so nice?" Enoch asked.

Enoch's grandfather said, "This tiger is from another time, another place. He once walked with me in the Garden. Somehow, some way, these children and Toby have come to us from beyond the ages."

The old man put one arm around Zonia and the other around Adam.

"And what are your names, my little ones?"

"I'm Zonia…he's Adam," Zonia said.

"Adam?" The grandfather looked at Adam, another tear trickling from the old man's eyes. "It is fitting that your name is Adam. The great Creator of all things has a way of saying what He wants to say."

"Is this the Time Before Noah?"

"Noah?" The old man looked puzzled. "I know of no such name."

Adam thought, *this must be the Time long before Noah was born.*

The grandfather felt there was great purpose within the visit by these two mysterious children. "Why have you come to us, little ones?"

"It's a Dream Doors Adventure. Part of Exploretime," Adam said.

"Dream Doors Adventure? Exploretime? What are these things?"

"It is part of my Exploretime learning. My sister has come along with me. It is my first time for Dream Doors."

"Learning? Who has sent you on this … *learning* experience?"

"The Great King does all things for us. The Great King wants us to know about many, many things," Adam said, his eyes growing wide with admiration as he thought about the Great King.

"The Great King deserves honor and glory!" Zonia put in enthusiastically.

The grandfather smiled and held the little girl close. "This Great King of yours sounds very familiar. Very much like someone…" he let the words die while smiling down at Zonia.

"What's *your* name?" Zonia asked.

"The same as your brother's name," the grandfather said.

"Adam?" she said.

The old man nodded. "But you may call me 'Grandfather'", he said, hugging her tightly.

"Are you the real Adam?" Zonia's brother asked, astonished at the realization.

"I *am* Adam, and I *am* real," the old man said with a hearty laugh. "That makes me the *real Adam*, I suppose!"

Adam Beam thought. The first man, he really is the first man! Adam could not express his amazement. He didn't know what to say to the first man. He and all the other children had heard and read so much about him

"There is much we must talk about, little ones. You are here for some grand thing! Let us make the most of your…how do you call it? Your Explore-time?" Grandfather Adam said with just a bit of mystery in his voice.

* * *

GRANDFATHER ADAM'S house looked surprisingly like houses in New Eden. It sat in a nest of flowers. Gigantic trees surrounded it. Its high walls were made of wide, cedar planks colored golden brown. Its windows were shuttered with strips of whitewashed wooden shutters, which were open so the cool breezes could flow through the house's big rooms, keeping the temperature just right.

Birds of every description, size and color fluttered in and out of the house. They often landed on Grandfather Adam's robed shoulders or on his outstretched finger and whistled to them.

Toby watched curiously, his whiskers twitching and his head and eyes jerking quickly, watching the little creatures fly about.

"Where is your ... your wife?" Adam asked. *If this was Adam, then what about Eve?* he wondered. He and his sister and the other children sat with the old man just outside the back of the house. They sat on rough-hewn chairs carved out of stone. Grandfather Adam touched Adam's cheek and smiled. Despite the smile, Adam saw sadness on the old man's face.

"Mother Eve has returned to the Maker of All Things," Grandfather Adam said quietly. "From where have you children come?"

"I've told you about Dream Doors, but I guess you don't know much about that," the boy said.

"No, I must say that I don't."

So then Adam told him all he knew about Dream

Doors. About Exploretime. About Glorainia and New Eden. He told Grandfather Adam about how he, Zonia and Toby lived in New Eden Time. How the Time before that was called the Trouble Time and the Time before that the Before Time. How they had been sent through the Dream Doors Adventure to this time—to Grandfather Adam's time—called the First Time.

Young Adam told about the Lightons, the Brightons, and Mrs. Levin. About the Wind Way. And most of all about the Great King, whose throne was in the sparkling, high-walled golden city that shimmered above the mountain that was Glorainia.

At the mention of the Great King, Grandfather Adam's face seemed to glow with light and his eyes sparked with great interest.

"And this Great King? Is he a *good* king? Do the people love him?"

"*He is the best of all kings!*" Zonia nearly shouted as if she could not believe anyone did not know *that*.

"There are more kings than *one* king?" the old man said, both amused and amazed by Zonia's exclamation.

"New Eden has many kings," Adam said. "But the Great King is the King of all Kings."

Grandfather Adam's face wore an expression of understanding.

"Where did you get that…what did you call it… that *thing* you wear around your waist?" Enoch asked.

"It's a dream doodler," Adam said. "It can draw

Dream Doors and dream drawings. It can make you disappear and appear again."

"The Great King has decreed that all children be allowed Dream Doors Adventures!" interjected Zonia. "My brother and I were given our Dream Doors Adventure in this First Time. That's why we're here." She put her arm around Toby's thick neck. "And Toby was allowed to come with us," she added joyfully.

Toby licked Zonia on her face, which brought the wrinkled nose and lip-curled frown as she wiped her face with her sleeve.

Grandfather Adam beckoned Adam and his sister with an outstretched hand. "Come to me, young ones. I believe I know why you were sent to me. I pray that your Great King has sent you to me."

The old man put his arms around Adam and Zonia. They listened to the story he had told and retold many, many times. Enoch and Grandfather Adam's grandchildren gathered close by, eager to again hear the story's telling.

"Grandmother Eve would be here today with all of us ..." he looked around at each of the children. "... if only we had obeyed." Again the grandfather's eyes filled with tears as he remembered. His voice became softer and sadder "She would have been as beautiful as the day she came to me in the Garden. If only we had obeyed."

"We were told by ... that is, Grandmother Eve and I ... were told by the Maker of All Things that everything in the Garden was ours to eat. Yes! All but the fruit which came from the Tree of the Knowledge of Good and Evil."

"I've heard that story lots of times!" Zonia said enthusiastically.

Enoch and the other children looked at Zonia, then at each other, surprised that she—this strange visitor—had heard the story they themselves had heard so many times.

"I thought as much," said the old man, gently hugging the girl. He looked at her brother, then again at her. "Then you know all the rest…how we could no longer stay in the Garden. About the poor animals that had to lose their lives to be sacrificed…for our disobedience. How we could no longer walk close to the Maker of All Things as before."

Grandfather Adam took a deep breath. When he spoke again, his words came with just a bit of anger in them.

"Here is something you do not know. Even the children of the … how do you call our time? The First Time? Even the children of the First Time do not know."

Enoch and the others looked at Grandfather Adam with puzzled expressions. They would listen carefully to this new thing he was about to tell.

"Before Mother Eve and I left the Garden, we were told to pick seven pieces of fruit. Seven apples from the Forbidden Tree. Seven lovely apples from the Tree of the Knowledge of Good and Evil."

The children of the First Time gasped in astonishment, their eyes wide with wonder. Grandfather Adam had never told them *this* part of the story!

"Yes … my children, the Maker told us to pick seven apples," the old man said, seeing the amazement on their faces.

"Mother Eve and I were told to keep the apples and to protect them no matter what. The Maker's messenger of light said that these seven apples were for some very special, important purpose."

"What purpose?" Enoch asked.

"We were not told, my son. We were told by the messenger of light only that the Evil One, who is the Deceiver, would desire to steal the apples, that he would want to keep the apples from being used for their great future purpose."

"Where are they now?" one of the granddaughters asked with great concern.

The old man again got a far away look in his eyes. "The messenger told me that I was to keep the apples with me at all times. Until the Maker sent for them."

Grandfather Adam looked very sad, his voice becoming soft. "I kept them with me always, knowing that the Evil One and his fellow evil ones, the slegna, would do their best to steal them. I was told that as long as I had the apples with me at all times, they could not be stolen. But that if I did not keep them with me…" The old man suddenly sounded angry with himself.

"But then I again disobeyed the Maker of All Things. It was just that one time. For many, many years I kept the apples safely with me at all times. It was just that *one* time."

"What happened?" Zonia asked.

"Late one evening when my work in the field was done for the day, I went to the well to draw water as I always did for Mother Eve." he paused for a big sigh of regret. "I pulled the sack with the seven apples from around my shoulder and put it down beside the well. About that time, Eve yelled to me. I ran to her, leaving the sack with the seven apples beside the well. When I got to her, a large serpent was coiled and had Mother Eve trapped against a pile of firewood. I drove the serpent away, then returned quickly to the well."

The children already knew the sorrowful end of the matter, but they listened intently while Grandfather Adam continued.

"When I got back to the well, the sack and the apples were gone. The slegna had stolen them."

"What did the Maker of All Things say?" another of the grandchildren asked.

"He is very loving and kind *always*. I asked his forgiveness for my disobedience. He forgave me, as always. But I cannot forgive myself. Those seven apples are of great future importance. Now they cannot be used by the Maker of All Things for his all-important purpose."

Adam Beam's eyes brightened as the thought came to him. "Grandfather Adam! I just remembered!"

"Yes, young one?"

"Zonia, Toby and I, not long after we began our Dream Doors Adventure, came to this strange forest where terrible creatures in black, hooded robes, surrounded us."

"And there was a hot, boiling pool, and Toby growled," Zonia said. "They were going to eat us! They said we were there to steal the apples, or something like that."

Grandfather Adam sat forward with great interest and surprise. "The slegna," he said, as if he were talking to himself.

"That's when I used the dream doodler," Adam said, patting the holster in which it rested against his right hip. "And then we were in the cave and after we came out of the cave, we saw Enoch and the other kids."

The old man smiled. All the children were glad that Adam's words had made their very-great-grandfather happy.

"Perhaps," Grandfather Adam said very thoughtfully, "yes, just perhaps the Maker of All Things who loves children so very, very much has chosen to use these little ones?" the old man said, again as if to himself.

"This...what do you call it... this dream doodler?" Grandfather Adam said with a raised eyebrow, looking at Adam Beam. "Tell me more about this instrument and what it can do."

Chapter 7

Toby sat beside Zonia, his head cocked curiously, his tail twitching while Adam Beam waved the dream doodler in the air after pressing the "DREAM DRAW" button. When a large dream drawing appeared in mid-air, Grandfather Adam and the children gathered behind him gasped, amazed.

"Once the dream drawing is painted in the air," Adam said, "we must hurry and step into it before it closes. The Dream Door doesn't stay open very long."

"And you say you first must *imagine* the drawing?" Grandfather Adam stroked the white whiskers on his chin while he thought about the amazing demonstration.

"Yes, sir. You just imagine what you want to be and what you want to do, and then when the dream drawing appears, you hurry through the Dream Door's portal."

"May I try it?" the old man asked

"Sure," Adam Beam handed it to Grandfather Adam.

"Now … let's see here…" Grandfather Adam held the dream doodler clumsily and fidgeted to try to remember how Adam had used it just seconds ago.

The boy, seeing the old man had forgotten, reached to point out the "DREAM DRAW" button.

"*Oh, yes.* I see now."

He held the dream doodler at arm's length, shut his eyes, and thought of the scene he wanted to dream draw. Suddenly, an image of a pasture appeared with several princely horses grazing on thick green grass.

"*Truly* amazing!" Grandfather Adam said. "And you say I can just walk right into that pasture?"

"Yes, sir. But you must hurry through the portal quickly. It closes really fast."

"May I try it again?" the old man said in a voice that expressed his delight.

"Sure, just remember you must imagine yourself back here when you are ready, and don't ever push that button." The boy pointed to the button marked "OUT".

"Why not?"

"Because that will take Zonia and me instantly back to the time and place we came from. That's why there is a covering over that button, so that it can't accidentally be pushed."

"Oh…I see."

Grandfather Adam again held the dream doodler at arm's length and depressed the "DREAM DRAW" button. Again, the scene of the grazing horses appeared.

The old man said, "Now I will just step through into the pasture."

But when he tried to step through the portal, he bounced off the dream drawing as if he were running into an invisible wall.

"What happened?" he asked, startled, and just a little bit shaken up. He, along with the children, watched the dream drawing disappear within just a few seconds.

"I … I don't know," Adam Beam said with a puzzled look. "Try it again."

Again, Grandfather Adam pointed the dream doodler, shut his eyes, and the scene appeared in midair. He walked to the picture and put one hand up against it, but his hand would not pass through. He bumped against the painting with one shoulder, but bounced off.

"I guess only Zonia, Toby and I can pass through," Adam Beam said. "Let me try it." Adam then imagined the same scene, and when it appeared he quickly passed through the door into the pasture. The portal closed behind him. Moments later, he reappeared in front of Grandfather Adam and the children.

"There's nothing wrong with the dream doodler," he said. "I guess it's just for Zonia, Toby and me."

The experience with the Dream Door drawing had tired Grandfather Adam, so he sat on a nearby stone, thinking. He sat silently for quite a long time, stroking his long white beard. "I am sure you have been sent to me to find the apples," he said to Adam Beam. "This *must* be the purpose for your coming to me."

The old man had the faraway look in his eyes. "The slegna have the apples. How, can you ever find them if I cannot go with you to show you the way?"

"Maybe *I* can go, Grandfather!" Enoch spoke up with enthusiasm. "Let me try it!"

Grandfather Adam looked at Adam Beam. "What do you think, young Adam?"

"Maybe no one from the First Time can go through the Dream Door portal?"

"Let me try," Enoch said. "Maybe we could go together through the door. Maybe at the same time."

"Let's try it," Adam Beam said, standing beside Enoch and pointing the dream doodler in the air. He shut his eyes and waved the instrument.

The same dream drawing the old man had painted in the air once again appeared. Both boys started through the opening at the same time. Adam Beam passed through easily. Enoch bounced off.

A few seconds later, Adam stepped out of thin air back into the presence of Grandfather Adam and the others. "I guess only Zonia, Toby and I can pass through the portals," Adam said, disheartened. He could see that Grandfather Adam and Enoch were as disappointed as he was.

"*There is one way.*" The voice inside Adam's head was the same he'd heard before. It was the voice of Zekor, the Lighton.

"What way?" Adam said out loud, causing all the others to look at him in a funny way. They could not hear the voice.

"He must be hearing the Lighton's voice," Zonia said, seeing the others' puzzled looks.

"*Imagine Enoch as already a part of the dream drawing,*" the voice said.

"Great! That's it!" Everyone watched Adam's face light up with the realization.

"What?" Enoch asked. "What's great?"

"I'll just imagine that you are already part of the scene and that way we can get you through the portal!" Adam said cheerfully.

Although he was not sure about what it all meant, Enoch was more than willing to do his part. "Let's do whatever you said."

"I'll imagine you into the dream drawing, then I will step through the portal, and then I will imagine you back here again."

Adam pointed the dream doodler and the scene with the pasture appeared. Only this time, Enoch appeared in the scene also, standing between the grazing horses. Adam stepped quickly through the portal, and the Dream Door closed.

Grandfather Adam, Zonia, Toby and the children looked around to see that Enoch had indeed vanished.

A few seconds later, Enoch appeared in front of them, a big smile on his face. Adam then stepped out of thin air into their presence. He, too, had a grin of delight. Now he knew how to get Enoch and the people of the First Time through a Dream Door.

* * *

GRANDFATHER ADAM SIPPED on the apple juice he poured himself and the children from the pitcher made of pottery. Adam Beam thought it tasted as good as the apple juice from the manna manger at home. The thought made him just a bit homesick to see Mom and Dad. But he couldn't let Zonia know he was homesick because she seemed to be doing just fine. The other children laughed and chitchatted happily as Grandfather Adam looked at the oldest of his granddaughters. "Ruth, will you please serve the honey cakes we made?"

"Yes, Grandfather," she said, and hurried into the next room from which the delicious smells were coming. She returned with a platter of light brown honey cakes, from which wisps of steam streamed upward.

"Thank you," Grandfather Adam said, kissing the girl on her cheek.

"These are just like Grandmother Eve used to make," the old man said, the glint of loving remembrance in his eyes. "*She* invented them!" he said with a chuckle.

The children, including Adam, Zonia and Enoch, sat around a large table of unfinished wood. It was stained by the spills of many such gatherings over the hundreds of years since Grandfather Adam had first made the table.

Toby sat between Adam and Zonia and his head stuck up well above the table top. He watched hungrily every time the cookie plate passed from one child to the next. Finally he snarled an impatient snarl.

"Ah! We've forgotten our striped friend," Grandfather Adam said with a laugh. "Someone give Toby Tiger a handful of honey cakes."

Adam Beam piled a number of the scrumptious cookie-like cakes in front of Toby, who quickly downed them.

"I am certain you have been sent to find the apples," Grandfather Adam said, looking at Adam from across the table. "But how? That is the question." The old man's eyes narrowed as he tried to think of how the mission could be accomplished.

"Maybe Toby could sniff them out and we could follow him," Zonia said in a serious tone. Toby cocked his head curiously toward Zonia when he heard his name and gave her a big lick on the side of her face.

"Toby could no doubt find them with his fine nose," the grandfather said with seriousness in his voice equal to that of Zonia's. "But where would he start? It has been several hundred years since they were stolen. Yet I know the apples can be found. They are to serve some great future purpose."

Grandfather Adam looked sad for not keeping the apples safe, knowing that he had once again disappointed the Maker of All Things.

"We'll find them, Grandfather!" Enoch said before taking a big bite of one of the honey cakes.

"But *how* to begin?" the old man said, rubbing his whiskers.

Adam Beam had been far too busy enjoying the most delicious dessert he had ever eaten to think about the task of finding the apples. But his sister had been thinking very hard on the matter. "Just use the dream doodler to imagine that we were there when the apples were stolen."

Grandfather Adam looked at Adam Beam, who looked back at him, and they both looked at Enoch. They all three looked at Zonia.

"Now I *know* she is the granddaughter of her Grandmother Eve! A wonderful, wonderful suggestion!" Grandfather Adam said. "Can the dream doodler do that?" he asked, looking at Adam.

"I don't know, but there is one sure way to find out," Adam said

"We must gather some food and water for you to take with you," Grandfather Adam said.

"We don't need to take food or water," Adam Beam said. "When we get hungry or thirsty, the dream doodler will provide whatever we need."

"A truly remarkable thing!" the old man said with a raised eyebrow. "The Maker of All Things be praised!"

Toby, enjoying being scratched behind his ears by Grandfather Adam, added a snarl of purring praise.

"Now, let's see…" Grandfather Adam walked slowly with the help of his walking stick. He pointed the stick toward some thick bushes. "The well was right about there." He jabbed the air with the stick to show Adam, Zonia and Enoch.

"Right there is where I was standing while I drew

water from the well. The water has of course long since dried up."

"And where was Grandmother Eve?" Enoch asked.

"She was near the old house, which was torn down more than 300 years ago."

The old man poked the walking stick in the direction of some large trees and just beyond them to an open field filled with beautiful flowers. "That serpent had her cornered. I left the well so quickly I forgot the sack of apples I had laid by the well before drawing water."

The old man put a hand on Adam Beam's shoulder and said, "Do you think you can go back to that time and place, young one?"

"I don't know...but I will sure try," the boy said with determination.

Grandfather Adam put his arms around both Adam Beam and Enoch. There was concern in his voice. "My children, there could be many dangers for you. But I am certain that the Maker of All Things will be with you as you search for the seven apples."

The old man looked at each of them, and Toby, and said, "Remember, the slegna, the ones you call the evols, have the powers of the Evil One. You must use the powers you've been given through the dream doodler very wisely as you seek out the seven apples from the Tree of Knowledge of Good and Evil."

Adam Beam said, "I will dream draw a Dream Door. You can tell me if it looks like the time and place that you drew water from the well."

He shut his eyes and imagined what the scene might look like in that time long ago. He pressed the "DREAM DRAW" button and the large dream drawing appeared in mid-air. The dream drawing was filled with fruit trees and birds and small creatures such as rabbits and squirrels, flying, hopping and scurrying about. At the center of the image stood a well made of stone with a small roof of wooden shingles atop thin poles. A single rope twined around another pole that stretched across the width of the well. This pole had a crank handle with which to lower and raise the bucket attached to the rope that hung straight down into the well.

Grandfather Adam stroked his beard and narrowed one eye. "That's almost right," he said. "But not quite."

"I don't think this will work unless we get it *exactly* right," Adam Beam said, and then he had an idea. He gave the Dream Doodler to Grandfather Adam and said, "You must remember the scene exactly as it was back then and then use the Dream Doodler to draw it."

"Very well!" the old man said, closing his eyes, remembering He waved the Dream Doodler in the air and a dream door portal opened. There was the well, and the sack of apples beside it.

Adam Beam studied the scene and fixed the image in his brain.

The Dream Door closed.

Quickly Adam took the Dream Doodler and

waved it in the air, remembering the image Grandfather Adam had drawn.

Another large Dream Door appeared. In this one appeared a much younger Grandfather Adam. He stood at the well. He took the sack of apples from around his shoulder and set it down beside the stones of the well.

"That's it!" Grandfather Adam said as the dream portal closed again. "That's exactly how I remember it."

"Great! Now all I have to do is imagine Enoch in the scene too and use the Disappear Dazzler Button. Everyone ready?"

The children nodded.

Adam closed is eyes, imagining the scene again, this time with Enoch in it. He waved the Dream Doodler pressing the green button.

The portal opened.

Quickly, Adam pressed the blue "DISAPPEAR DAZZLER" button and he, Zonia and Toby jumped through the dream door.

* * *

ADAM, Zonia and Enoch watched the man draw water from the well. Toby cocked his head curiously and snarled a quiet snarl of curiosity.

"*Ssshh*," Adam said in a whisper to Toby, patting him on the head. They were invisible now, but could still be heard. They must remain quiet.

The young man at the well was tall and straight,

and had a strange but beautiful glow that seemed to surround him while he cranked the rope that drew the bucket full of water upward. The dark brown sack by the well had to be the sack with the seven apples, those the Maker of All Things had told Adam to always keep with him no matter what.

The beauty that surrounded the three children and Toby far exceeded that of the time from which they had just come. The trees hung heavy with fruit of every color and size. The small animals that fluttered or hopped about seemed to have no fear of the man as they gathered around him. Some of them clung to his shoulders. One squirrel even sat atop his head while he drew the water. The birds, too, flew about the young, strong man while he worked, and he talked to them in an almost whistling language. They seemed to understand.

The peacefulness suddenly shattered when a cry rang out in the distance.

"*Help! Adam!*" the female voice screamed while Adam dropped the bucket of water and began running toward the woman.

"*Let's follow him!*" Zonia said in an excited whisper.

"No. We must watch the sack of apples," Enoch said, his eyes trained upon the dark sack that lay crumpled next to the stone well. Seconds later, the birds who had been chirping about happily suddenly could no longer be seen or heard. Rabbits and the other creatures that had been playing about the feet of Adam before he heard Eve's call scurried into the bushes. All was silent and still while Adam, Zonia, Enoch and Toby watched the sack of apples.

"Let's just go get them now and leave with them," Zonia said.

Adam thought the idea sounded reasonable. "Yes…that would keep them from being stolen," he said in a whisper.

Before Adam, Zonia, Enoch and Toby started for the sack of apples, Adam heard the familiar voice in his head again.

"*No, Adam,*" the Lighton's voice said. "*If you take the apples, then you will have stolen them from Adam, who was told to keep them with him at all times.*"

"Hold it! We can't take the apples because they haven't been stolen yet. If we took them, *we* would be the ones stealing them."

Enoch and Zonia thought on Adam's words for a moment. Toby interrupted their thoughts with a snarl when he sensed an evil presence.

Suddenly several spirit-like beings appeared in the air. They floated silently to the well and hovered over the sack containing the apples. Deep, sinister, cackling laughter came from within the black hoods.

The children, invisible to the evols, watched while the eerie creatures opened the sack and peered inside. They laughed again, their horrible cackling shaking the very air surrounding the children.

The evols slowly faded, finally becoming invisible. But the bag with the apples did not vanish; rather, it began floating away.

"They are taking the apples!" Enoch said,

pointing at the sack, which was now whisking through the air faster and faster.

"*Hurry*! Let's follow it. We can't let the apples get away!" Adam commanded, running in the direction the sack was flying.

"It's no use. We can't keep up," Adam said after a few moments of chasing the flying sack.

The children stopped to catch their breath. Toby ran on ahead a little ways and stopped to look back at them, wondering why they had given up.

"What are we going to do? They're getting away with the apples!" Enoch said, watching the sack get smaller and smaller as it flew away from them.

Adam had to think of something fast!

Chapter 8

ADAM REMEMBERED A HISTORY LESSON HE'D LEARNED in Exploretime. It was about the time when The Great King returned to earth at the end of the Trouble Times. The Great King and all the Brightons came riding through the clouds on great white horses – horses that flew from heaven to earth.

Adam imagined three of those horses now, with Enoch sitting on the back of one of them. He closed his eyes and waved the Dream Doodler in the air and a dream portal opened up before their eyes.

"Quick, Zonia!" He grabbed her hand and leaped through the portal. Two of the gleaming white horses went down on their knees so that the children could climb onto their backs. Toby jumped up behind Zonia.

"Follow that sack!" Adam shouted.

In an instant the horses leaped into the air. The

children held onto their flowing manes as the horses flew like a mighty wind.

They flew faster and faster as the sack of apples flew faster and faster some distance in front of them, but they could not gain on the sack as the evols dove into a forest. The evil ones flew ever faster between the thick trunks of the trees.

The powerful horses flew swifter than birds, twisting and turning around and between the tree trunks while keeping the sack of apples in their view. The children held on tighter and tighter.

They suddenly burst into an opening, still following the sack. It flew straight toward the rocky side of a mountain. Without slowing down, the sack slammed into the mountainside.

The gleaming white horses flew to the ground and landed in a gallop and then stopped where the crumpled sack lay at the bottom of the mountain wall the children and the tiger jumped down off the horses backs and the three horses disappeared in a bright sparkle of green light

"That was exciting, and a little scary," Zonia said.

"I like being Dream Doodled," Enoch said, smiling.

Adam picked up the sack and looked inside. As he suspected, the sack was empty. "They are not here!" he said, showing the open sack to his companions.

Enoch said, "They must have passed right through the rock."

"Then why didn't the sack pass through, too?" Zonia said.

Toby sniffed the sack and snarled a puzzled snarl.

"What do we do? We will never find the apples now," Enoch said.

"We will find them. They can't get away from us that easily," Adam said, but he didn't know what to do either.

"Look!" Zonia pointed to a long, narrow crack between two rocks. "I think it's a cave entrance. This must be how the Evols took the apples into the mountain."

Adam squeezed through the crack and Zonia and Enoch followed.

Zonia squinted. "I can't see *anything*. It's too dark. We need flashlights."

Adam dream doodled a drawing and Zonia and Adam reached into the portal to get two of the three flashlights Adam's imagination and the dream doodler had produced. But when Enoch tried to reach through the portal, his hand bounced off.

"I'll get it for you," Zonia said, reaching inside the portal to get the other flashlight. She handed it to Enoch and instructed him on the flashlight's use.

Together the three searched the cave as their bright flashlight beams moved around the jagged rocks along the walls. Deeper and deeper they went until they were far inside the mountain.

"Look! Over here!" Zonia said, pointing.

Stalactites and stalagmites grew from the ceiling and from the floor of the cavern to form columns where they joined together. An eerie red glow illuminated the columns and the dark shadowy walls of rugged rock formations. The glow coming from somewhere deep from the cavern pulsed with life almost as if this region beneath the mountain had a heartbeat.

Adam could see the worry on Enoch's face, and Zonia didn't look exactly happy, either.

"The Great King is always with us," Adam said in a strong, confident voice. "Nothing can hurt us in a Dream Doors Adventure," He added, a little uncertain.

Rumbling sounds in the distance caused Adam to put his hands up and ask for quiet.

"*Ssshh*… listen…."

The sound grew a bit louder, but then stopped.

"It came from that direction," Enoch said, pointing toward the place beyond the stalactites and stalagmites.

Because they could not see beyond the dark columns, they walked between them toward the blackness. They shined their flashlight beams together into the cavern's darkest region.

"It's so dark!" Zonia exclaimed.

They kept walking very slowly. Their lights revealed only the sandy floor and darkness beyond.

"This cave must go back a long way. It doesn't seem to have any walls or ceiling." Adam said, shining his beam of light all around the inside of the cavern. The beam revealed nothing.

Again, the rumbling sound grew louder for a few moments, then quieted. The sand on which they walked became deeper the farther they walked. They had to lift their legs higher and higher to step upon and over the small sand dunes.

All at once, the sand beneath their feet began to shake. They tried to keep from falling. The shaking got stronger. Toby snarled a snarl of surprise and the children yelled loud, startled yells when suddenly the sand began swirling downward, pouring into the floor of the cave.

Downward, downward they went, tumbling and rolling one on top of the other. They seemed to do somersaults forever while they and the sand poured faster and faster into the unknown.

Although the suddenness of their fall took their breath, Adam, Zonia, Enoch and Toby landed softly. They sat for a few seconds on the piles of sand.

"Is everybody okay?" Adam asked, brushing the sand from his hair and from his shirt.

"I'm okay," Zonia said, brushing herself off.

Enoch sat spitting sand from his mouth.

Toby snarled an irritated snarl, then stood and shook as hard as he could shake, flinging the grit from his fur in all directions.

They slid down the steep pile of sand until they stood on the hard surface of their new surroundings. Adam retrieved the shinning flashlights half buried in the sand and the adventurers moved deeper into the new, underground region.

"Toby has found something over there!" Zonia said, pointing. The tiger poked his head and body halfway through an opening along one wall.

They followed the cat into the newfound passageway. This new cavern was even larger than the previous one. Stalactites and stalagmites formed columns like in the other cavern, but these were larger. Much larger. As big around as the gigantic trees of the outside world.

A red-orange glow lit the entire cavern. But still there were the dark places. Weird shadows flickered across the walls and in the distance as far as they could see. Bubbling, gurgling sounds seemed to come from somewhere in the darkness.

"This place is scary," Zonia said, shivering.

"Don't worry. I'll Dream Doodle us out of here if it gets too scary. Adam reached for the Dread Doodler.

"*The dream doodler!*"

Adam looked down at the dream doodler holster, then felt it with his hand. *Gone!* Probably lost in the sand when they tumbled through the floor above. "I've lost the dream doodler!"

"Oh no!" Zonia cried.

"Let's go look for it," Adam said. "It's probably back there in the sand."

They turned back to the hole through which they had just come.

"Is this what you are looking for?" a screechy voice asked with a cackle of laughter.

Adam gasped as the creatures slowly materialize. A black hooded evol floating in air held the dream doodler in its long, bony hand. Several more evols appeared, surrounding the children. Toby, who growled and bared his fangs.

Before the tiger could attack, a semitransparent, yellowish barrier of some sort surrounded him.

"That takes care of your striped friend," the evol who held the dream doodler said. "And now it is time to take care of YOU!"

"COME!" the evol who held the dream doodler screamed. His screeching command made the whole cavern shake.

Adam, Zonia, Enoch and Toby heard scuffing sounds that grew louder and louder. Three huge, hideous creatures with large, bulging red eyes shuffle into view and surrounded the children. They looked half human and half lizard.

"*Mutons!*" Enoch whispered so that only Adam and Zonia could hear. Toby roared angrily from the nearly invisible cage and raked at the yellowish walls with his powerful claws.

The mutons' skin was pinkish-gray. They had no hair on their bumpy, bone-ridged heads. Their wide jaws hung partially open, showing big sharp teeth. Thick red tongues partly stuck out between their teeth. Their long, hairy arms caused their hands to drag the ground when they walked. Their short, thick, bowed legs made them appear to limp. They shuffled their web-toed feet when the moved.

"Take the human children and put them with the others!" the evol said. The mutons began growling and gnashing their sharp teeth.

"Nothing can hurt children during a Dream Doors Adventure," Adam said out loud.

"Oh, you think not?" The evol laughed and look

at the Dream Doodler in his hand. "Without your clever toy, you're helpless."

* * *

THE MUTON GIANTS shuffled along behind Adam, Zonia, and Enoch. The ugly, half-human, half-evol beasts grunted and growled, and made the children hurry along the dark, rocky tunnel.

Finally, they came to an opening in one wall of the tunnel. One of the mutons glared at Adam and pointed a gnarled finger at the opening, grunting.

"I guess he wants us to go through there," Adam said, leading the way.

This cavern was far larger than even the big one with the stalactites and stalagmites. Boiling, gurgling sounds, along with the rumbles of rockslides and the hissing of steam, filled their ears while they moved along in front of the shuffling mutons.

"We must be in the center of the mountain," Adam said, looking around at the glowing cavern. Puffs of steam shot up from the floor in the distance. Here dozens of the giants moved about. The beasts carried stones, boiled lava in big buckets, and did other muton tasks.

"Those things are everywhere," Zonia whispered in a disgusted tone.

The mutons behind the children nudged them onward. They came to a long, gorge-like trench that separated one part of the cavern floor from the other.

One of the mutons pointed at a rickety wooden bridge, which stretched across the chasm.

"They want us to cross that bridge," Enoch said. "I don't think it will hold both us and them."

The children stepped at first very cautiously upon the swaying wooden bridge. They held to the thick rope handrails. The bridge swayed and seemed to buckle and stretch as they moved.

The mutons did not follow onto the bridge, but growled and grunted orders from their side of the chasm. They pointed and made hand gestures commanding the children to cross to the other side where other beasts waited for them.

Once across, these giants forced the children along a deep, grooved pathway past other staring mutons.

The children had to carefully step around pools of bubbling lava and pits that vented steam. Soon they came to another hole in one of the walls of the cave. This hole had long metal rods that stretched from top to bottom, spaced close together to form bars.

The bars lifted up into the top of the cave. The mutons grunted and pointed for the children to go into the hole. The bars lowered, locking the children in a dark prison cell.

Adam, Zonia and Enoch looked at their shadowy surroundings. They heard muffled voices, which told them they were not alone.

Children!

"*Who are you?*" Adam said, moving closer to the children, huddled together in the semidarkness.

The little ones looked at Adam, Zonia and Enoch. They were obviously frightened.

"I'm Adam, and this is Zonia," Adam said, putting his hand on his sister, then on Enoch. "This is Enoch."

Like always, there were no language barriers for children of New Eden. First Time children, Trouble Time children—it made no difference. The Great King granted that talk between New Eden children and all others would have no limitations or boundaries. These frightened children understood perfectly —as easily as did Enoch.

"We won't hurt you. We are here to help you."

Adam spoke bravely. He did not know why he told these children that he, Zonia and Enoch had come to help them. He only knew it was true.

"I am Seth," the oldest of the boys among the children said. He seemed uncertain of how much he could trust these just-arrived prisoners.

The boy introduced the other children, all his brothers and sisters. And after a few minutes of getting acquainted, Seth's brothers and sisters seemed most curious about the strange clothing Adam and Zonia wore. They were particularly fascinated with the belt and empty holster around Adam's waist.

The girls touched the material of Zonia's shirt while the boys moved their fingertips over the bumps and ridges of the belt and holster. Several of the children seemed fascinated by the strange shoes Zonia and her brother wore.

Adam said, "How did you get here? Why are you locked up like this?"

"The Fallen Ones took us from our home yesterday while we slept," Seth said. "I don't know why. All I know is that one of the Fallen Ones kept saying over and over, 'Steal the seed and change the future.'"

"Steal the seed and change the future?" Adam repeated, trying to make sense of the words. "Don't be afraid. We'll get you out of here, he said with courage in his voice."

Enoch and Zonia were not so confident as a hideous muton, more than 10 feet tall, shuffled up to the bars to gawk at them. The creature snapped his powerful jaws and ground his horrible teeth.

"That one is the key keeper," Seth whispered. "I think he would like to eat us, but the evil ones told him never to touch us."

"He sleeps a lot," one of Seth's sisters said softly. "He snores so loud it shakes the whole cave."

The muton hissed and growled, and its bulging eyes seeming to grow a brighter red. The monster sat by the bars and leaned against the rock surface of the cave. Within seconds, its eyes disappeared behind the folds of its drooping eyelids. Its massive head nodded forward until its broad chin rested against its fat chest, and he began to snore. The snoring did indeed shake the cave cell.

"See? told you," Seth's sister said, almost with amusement in her voice.

"Do you know anything about the apples?" Adam asked Seth.

"You mean the seven apples my father keeps with him at all time?"

"Your father?" Adam blinked, startled by the boy's answer.

"Grandfather Adam is *your* father?" Enoch said, equally startled by Seth's question.

"Grandfather Adam? Who is he?" Seth said looking puzzled.

"We've got to figure a way to get that key from the muton," Adam said, interrupting the confusing matter of Adam being father or grandfather. He didn't understand the puzzle any better than did Enoch or Seth, but he did know they could not spend a lot of time worrying about it.

"How can we get that key?" he whispered, mostly to himself.

"The apples. What about the apples?" Zonia said, trying to get the conversation on the right track again.

"The apples are for some great purpose!" another of Seth's sisters said enthusiastically. "They are from the Garden of long ago."

"My father told us that the seven apples are the only things left from the Garden of long ago," Seth said.

His sister corrected him. "The seven apples, as well as he and mother, are the only things left that came from the Garden."

One of Seth's younger brothers said timidly, "The

Maker of All Things told Father that the apples are to be used for some great eternal purpose."

The children's conversation was interrupted by several noisy snorts from the sleeping muton.

Adam said, "We have just got to get out of here, find those apples, and get them back."

Adam thought and thought about how to get out of the cave cell. He sat near the bars, looking at the snoring muton leaning against the cave wall just beyond them. There seemed no way out. The key to the cell door hung on a hook attached to a belt around the beast's waist.

"What kind of creatures are mutons?" Adam asked Seth.

"They are the children of the fallen ones. The muton's fathers are the fallen ones. Their mothers are humans," Seth said.

"You call them fallen ones. Enoch calls them slegna. And we are taught that they are evols. I think that they are all the same," Adam said, looking at the snoring, drooling muton.

"I suppose," Seth said, letting some of the sand he had picked up from the cave floor sift through his fingers.

Adam studied the big key hanging from the muton's side, watching it rise and fall with each breath the muton took. When the beast snorted, the key sometimes jumped with the quick movement.

"Why have they brought you here?" Adam said.

"I don't know. I only know that one of the fallen

ones kept saying, 'Steal the seed and change the future.'"

"It must have something to do with them stealing the apples," Adam said.

Both boys jumped when the muton suddenly jerked his whole body in what must have been part of a nightmare.

"Look! The key fell off the hook!" Adam said, getting to his knees and crawling closer to the muton, who settled back into sleep just outside the bars.

The key had fallen several inches away from the creature's leg. Adam moved as closely to the bars as he could. He stretched his arm between them all the way to his shoulder and crawled his fingers through the sand toward the key, but the key was just out of reach.

"Your arms are longer than mine, Seth," Adam said. "See if you can get the key."

Seth reached between the bars and was able to rake the key toward himself with the longest of his outstretched fingers.

"Great!" Adam whispered excitedly.

Seth handed Adam the key.

"We will have to be very quiet," Adam said. He reached between the bars and quietly put the key into the lock. When he turned the key, the door lock clicked loudly.

Both boys looked at the muton giant when he spasmed against the rock wall where he sat. His eyes opened and he made smacking sounds. He shifted where he sat on the sandy cave floor and rubbed one of his gnarled hands over his face, then let the hand drop heavily to the floor. His eyelids drooped, then plopped shut, covering the red eyes.

Adam and Seth knelt beside the bars, afraid to move. The muton could awaken at any moment!

Finally, the beast began snoring steadily again. Adam whispered to Seth, "Tell them to be very quiet. We're getting out of here."

Chapter 9

ONE BY ONE THE CHILDREN TIPTOED PAST THE
snoring muton. They crept quietly along the dark wall
of the tunnel. Adam led the way. They heard shouting
and shrieking behind them. The evols were screaming
at the muton who had let the children escape. There
was the rumble of heavy footsteps.

Adam put up his hand and the children stopped.

A number of mutons rushed by them just outside
the tunnel.

"They're looking for us," Adam whispered. "I've
got to find the dream doodler. It's our only chance."

"But how?" Zonia asked in an excited whisper.
"There's no telling where those evols hid it."

"There's got to be a way, there's just got to,"
Adam said.

"Let's ask the Great King to help us," Zonia said.

Enoch whispered, "Who is the Great King?"

"You call Him the Maker of All Things," Adam said.

"The Maker of All Things!" Seth chimed in. "He is your Great King?"

"*Ssshh!*" Adam said putting a finger to his lips.

The shuffling sounds grew louder and louder as mutons searched everywhere. The evols flew about the caverns, desperate to find the children. Although the small, dark tunnel for the moment hid them from the evil ones, it was just a matter of time. Adam determined that it was indeed time to call upon the Great King.

He shut his eyes and thought of the great, majestic King who was always with them, no matter what, no matter where.

Zonia, too, joined him in his thoughts. Together they called out to His Majesty, who heard from across the vast ages and answered from within the children's own minds.

"*Push the button you will find just inside the buckle of the belt around your waist, Adam.*"

Adam and Zonia, heard the voice clearly. Adam quickly opened the clasp of the belt. *Yes! There it was!*

He pressed the button and instantly felt a thump against his right leg.

"The dream doodler!" he said, much louder than he meant to. He pulled it from its holster and held it tightly. The Great King had answered their prayer! Now they must find Toby and the seven apples.

The sounds of footsteps grew louder and louder.

The evols and the mutons had found the tunnel and were coming after them!

"*Hurry*! This way!" Adam shouted. The children followed him quickly through the tunnel toward a red glowing light ahead.

A few seconds later they stood at the tunnel's opening. A large flow of red-hot lava moved along the floor of the cavern into which the tunnel led. The lava's glow gave off enough light so they could easily see to walk safely through the cavern. There was no time to move slowly. The approaching giants were close behind them.

"They are going to catch us!" Zonia shouted to be heard above the muton's movements and the boiling, steaming lava noises.

"I'll take care of that!" Adam said, pointing the dream doodler back at the tunnel opening that he, Zonia and the children had just left. He shut his eyes and imagined rock falling, then pressed the "DREAM DRAW" button and waved the dream doodler at the cave opening. The wall around and above the tunnel began to crack and rumble. Within seconds, the cave opening crumbled and fell, covering the exit.

"That ought to hold them," Adam said, leading the children farther into the cavern.

"There's no way out of here," Enoch said, examining their surroundings.

"Yes, there is," Adam said, shouting loud enough for Enoch to hear over the boiling noise.

"I'm going to dream draw you and the other kids to the outside of this mountain to the place where we found the sack when the evols went through the mountain. You and the others stay right there until we come for you. You and Seth take care of the other children. Keep them there, okay?"

Enoch nodded.

Adam shut his eyes and imagined the exact spot where the empty sack had fallen to the ground just outside the mountain's rocky wall. He imagined the children standing there and pressed the "DREAM DRAW" button. The children vanished from the cavern and instantly appeared in the dream drawing. A few seconds later, the Dream Door portal closed and then the scene disappeared.

Suddenly three evols materialized near the tunnel's collapsed opening. They gave an ear-piercing shriek as flew toward Adam and Zonia, their white, bony fingers outstretched from beneath the sleeves of their black hooded robes.

Adam pressed the "DISAPPEAR DAZZLER" button and winked out of sight.

The evols were furious. They flew back and forth across the cavern, desperately searching for the vanished children. The mutons broke through the rocks that covered the tunnel's opening and hurried about the cavern, grunting and howling, but no one could find Adam and his sister.

Crouched against the cave wall, Adam shut his eyes and imagined Toby in the yellow cage. He pressed the "DREAM DRAW" button and he and Zonia leaped through the portal which instantly opened.

They were still invisible when they stepped through the Dream Door into the room where Toby lay inside the yellowish transparent cage.

They became visible again. Adam pointed the dream doodler at Toby and imagined him outside the cage. The tiger vanished, then reappeared just in front of the children. He growled a growl of approval and nuzzled the children, extremely happy to see them again.

Noises from behind startled them. They turned to face a hoard of angry mutons, racing toward them.

"Quick! Do something!" Zonia cried.

"Watch this!" Adam said, pointing the dream doodler at the gigantic creatures. He shut his eyes and pressed the button.

All six of the beasts disappear. Adam and Zonia turned at the sound of growling and howling coming from behind them. The mutons were inside the yellow transparent cage Toby had been just seconds before.

"Quantum!" Zonia said, clapping.

The mutons beat on the side of the cage, their red eyes bulging, their thick, purple tongues thrusting between their gnashing, knife-sharp teeth.

"Now let's get out of here!" Adam said.

"What about the apples?" Zonia said. "We've got to find the apples!"

* * *

ADAM, Zonia and Toby stepped through the portal of the dream drawing, but not before Adam first pressed the "DISAPPEAR DAZZLER" button, making himself, his sister and the tiger invisible.

The cave room into which Adam had dream doodled them was very dark except for the ball of pale yellow light.

"The apples!" Zonia whispered. "They're inside that a glowing ball!" The apples were arranged in a circle on top of a large pedestal and surrounded by a ball of yellowish light, like the force field that had held Toby. She looked around at their darkened surroundings. "Let's just get them and get out of here,"

Adam pulled the dark sack from his belt where it had been since he picked it up just outside the mountain. He held the dream doodler toward the glowing light. He imagined the seven apples being inside the sack he held with his other hand.

He pushed the "DREAM DRAW" button. Nothing happened! He tried again and still nothing happened. The seven apples remained on the pedestal tabletop surrounded by the glowing ball of light.

"What's wrong?!" Zonia said.

"It must be a different kind of force field from the one that held Toby," Adam said. "It won't let the apples pass through it."

Toby growled a curious growl.

"What are we going to do?" Zonia asked.

Adam started to answer, but strange noises that grew louder and louder stopped him. He pulled on Zonia's arm, urging her to come with him into one dark corner. Several evols suddenly appeared near the glowing ball of light. They floated in the air and talked angrily to each other, their evil voices echoing from the walls of the cave.

"The Magnificent One is most displeased. He will not deal lightly with us for allowing the human children to escape!" one of the evols said.

The yellowish light of the force field made the hooded figures appear eerier than usual. Several more evols materialized and floated nearby.

"His Magnificence does not understand that the children of the Future Time have some great power given them by the Maker of All Things," the evol said in a whiny, voice. "His Magnificence will just have to be made to realize..."

The cave became blindingly bright. Adam, Zonia and even Toby had to squint to keep the light from hurting their eyes.

"His Magnificence will have to be made to realize what?" The deep voice made the whole cave room quake. Chunks of stone cracked and fell from the ceiling.

The brightness dimmed a little and took on the form of a huge fan-shaped being.

"A Lightons!" Zonia whispered.

It was a Lightons like none other Adam had seen in New Eden. He was gigantic. His eyes were golden in color and pulsed with sparks of bright light when he spoke.

The evols, fell to their knees, bowing before him.

"You cannot be trusted to guard even small children," His Magnificence said, his booming voice shaking the cave room. "Should you be trusted to keep the apples from fulfilling their purpose?"

One of the evols raised his hooded head. "Your Magnificence, we shall find the children and they shall never have the apples."

"*SILENCE!*" His iridescent eyes flashed like lightning. More pieces of rock tumbled to the floor.

"Do you fools not know that the children of New Eden are right here among you?" the Lightons said in a calmer voice.

The evols looked around the room.

"Uh-oh!" Adam whispered, putting his arm around his sister to protect her.

Toby snarled an angry, protective snarl.

Chapter 10

"WHERE IS THE INSTRUMENT THAT YOU BROUGHT WITH you from Future Time?" The evol asked angrily, pointing at the empty holster on Adams side. The creature floated just outside the glowing ball of light that held Adam, Zonia and Toby captive within the same kind of force field that held the apples. "Tell me!" the evol screeched.

"I don't know," Adam said. "I must have lost it somewhere."

"No!" the enraged evol screamed. "We would have found it by now if you had lost it!"

Adam really did not know what had happened to the dream doodler. It had been in the holster a moment before the gigantic Lighton had with one wave of his huge shining hand, made the children visible, and with yet another wave, put the force field around Adam, Zonia and the tiger, and then in a blinding brilliance, disappeared.

"We will find it no matter where you've hidden it! We will find it!!"

The evols put their heads together and spoke quietly, and then passed through a solid rock wall, leaving Adam, Zonia and Toby imprisoned within the glowing ball.

"Now what are we going to do?" Zonia asked.

Toby snarled a questioning snarl.

"We are here for a reason?" Adam said, putting an arm around his sister to comfort her. "The Great King is with us always."

"Nothing can hurt children who are in a Dream Doors Adventure," Zonia said in a weak, trembling voice, trying to reassure herself.

Adam said, "Don't be frightened, Zonia. We will be home again before you know it."

Adam peered through the glowing force field barrier at the seven apples upon the pedestal, surrounded in their own shimmering ball of light. They must free themselves, get the apples, and rescue the children waiting for them outside the mountain. *But how?* How could they possibly do it without … he put his hand on the holster.

The dream doodler?

He looked down at the holster. It *looked* empty, yet he could feel the dream doodler's handle!

It was invisible!

He pulled the invisible instrument from its holster, feeling its ridges and bumps. "*Yes!*"

"Look Zonia! It's the dream doodler!"

"I don't see anything," she said, as if Adam had lost his mind.

Toby cocked his head and sniffed Adam's hand.

"Here. Feel."

Zonia touched the hard surface of the dream doodler. "It's invisible! *Quantum!*"

"The Great King must have made it invisible so the evols couldn't take it away from me," Adam silently thanked the Great King. But how to use the dream doodler? He had tried before to get the apples from behind the glowing ball force field, or whatever it was.

It couldn't hurt to try it again. He closed his eyes and imagined him and Zonia outside of their force field prison.

When he pushed the "DREAM DRAW" button, nothing happened. The dream doodler could not get them past the barrier!

We have to think of a way," Adam said.

"Maybe you should push the "OUT" button?" Zonia suggested.

"Then we would have failed in our mission. The Great King and Grandfather Adam are depending on us. There's got to be another way."

Zonia sat on the floor and rested her chin on her fist. "If only we hadn't gotten in this fix in the first place," she said.

Adam was pacing. He stopped suddenly and looked at her, an idea growing in his brain. "That's it, Zonia. You're brilliant."

"What did I say?" she asked, looking up in surprise.

"We'll dream doodle us back in time before we got into this mess." Adam shut his eyes and imagined with all his might that he, Zonia and Toby were standing in this room back in time, just before the evols had put the force field around the seven apples.

He first pushed the blue "DISAPPEAR DAZZLER" to make them invisible, and then the green button and waved the dream doodler in the air. Instantly the dream drawing appeared in front of them. "Hurry through the portal!"

In the flash of a second they stood within the room invisible to the evols. One of them was arranging the apples in a circle on top of the pedestal.

Adam knew what he had to do next. He dream doodled the apples into the sac and then imagined the scene just outside the mountain where the children awaited. He pushed the green "DREAM DRAW" button again. A portal opened and the children and Toby jumped through it.

Startled, the evols flew toward them, screaming angrily. When the first evol tried to go through the portal, it bounced off. The other evols crashed into him from behind. The portal closed and the drawing vanished.

* * *

TOBY LED THE WAY, jumping from the Dream Door

portal onto the grass and earth where Enoch, Seth and the others were supposed to be waiting. Adam and Zonia followed right behind the tiger landing feet first in the thick grass. They looked around. The children were nowhere to be seen.

"I think we are still back in time a little bit," Adam said, remembering that he had dream doodled them back in time and had not yet dream doodled them forward again.

Zonia said, "Just imagine where they are right now, then make a drawing so we can join them."

Adam had already begun doing just that. As the dream drawing appeared in midair, Adam, Zonia and Toby watched in wide-eyed wonderment. Muton giants stomped angrily around the small opening the children had used to enter the cave. The opening was much too small for the huge half-man, half-evol monsters to go through. But they very much wanted to get into the cave for some reason. The mutons pulled at the big boulders surrounding the cave opening. They were able to remove only a few of the smaller stones. They beat on the larger rocks with their fists and grunted and growled in a rage.

"It's the kids!" Adam exclaimed. "We've got to help them!"

Adam jumped into the drawing through the Dream Door portal, followed closely by his sister and the tiger. He pushed the "DISAPPEAR DAZZLER" button on the bottom of the dream doodler's handle and the three of them became invisible.

Now the muton giants were taking away larger and larger pieces of stone from the cave opening. Within a few seconds, they would be able to get to the children within the cave. Adam heard the kids screaming and crying while the beasts grunted and growled as they did their work.

"I'll take care of this," Adam said boldly. He pointed the dream doodler at the mutons and imagined as hard as he could imagine.

A loud, growling roar shook the whole area. The mutons stopped their clawing at the stones surrounding the cave opening and turned to look at the gargantuan beast that had made the ear-shattering noise.

A gigantic tyrannosaurus stood above the mutons, its massive jaws with eight-inch-long, razor-sharp teeth chewed up and down. The great tyrant lizard roared again. Its shorter front legs clawed at the air while its tree-sized tail swooshed back and forth along the ground.

"Did you do *that*?!" Zonia asked, her eyes wide in disbelief.

"It's only my imagination, but the mutons don't know that," Adam said with a chuckle.

Sure enough, the mutons, their red eyes almost popping out of their ugly heads, scurried about, flailing their long, hairy arms trying to get away from the dinosaur.

The mutons crashed into each other or into trees while they fled the terrifying image. Within seconds all mutons had vanished into the forest.

"*Quantum!*" was the only thing Zonia could think to say.

Toby snarled an amazed but totally pleased snarl.

* * *

"THAT IS the way to our home," Seth said, pointing toward a narrow opening between the rocky cliffs.

With Seth leading the way, Adam, Zonia, Toby, Enoch and all of the other children moved through the narrow pathway. It soon opened to an area high above a wide valley.

The region was much more beautiful than the one they had just left. It seemed as if it were an entirely different land altogether. Rivers and lakes and lush green forests filled the valley below. Adam could see in Seth's face that he was happy to be home.

The giggling, cheerful noises coming from the other children made Zonia know that they, too, were joyful to once again see their homeland.

Suddenly, a brilliant, blinding flash of light burst in front of the children! They gasped with surprise. The brilliance dimmed until it became a familiar form.

"*A slegna!*" Seth said in an astonished voice.

The twenty-foot-tall, human-like figure of light straddled the pathway. His arms were folded over his chest while his laser-like eyes sparked with anger.

"And where do you young foolish ones think you are going?" the slegna said in an echoing voice of hatred, holding the children transfixed with its golden eyes.

"I would like you to meet my … pet," the golden eyes sparked. "And I would like him to meet you. Or perhaps I should say I would like him to EAT you. Because he is, you see, quite hungry."

The 20-foot-tall figure of light vanished and in his place appeared an even bigger creature; a massive, greenish, snake-like beast with four legs and long sharp claws. Its head was that of a dragon with ruby eyes and a great mouth full of knife-blade-like teeth. When it opened its mouth, and roared long, hot flickers of red and yellow flame shot toward the children, who backed away and huddled together.

The dragon's long, spiked tail whipped back and forth as it shook its head and clawed the earth with great, curved talons. Its slit eyes blinked and its nostrils flared with each roar it made.

Toby crouched as if to attack, his tiger fur standing up on his back.

"*Toby! No!*" Adam yelled. "You can't stop that thing!"

Toby dashed to one side. He seemed to be trying to lure the beast away from the children. The dragon shot flames in his direction. Toby was too fast. He leaped out of the way before the flames could reach him.

"*Use the dream doodler, Adam,*" It was Zekor's voice inside Adam's mind. "*You cannot make the beast disappear. It is the creation of the Evil One. You must instead imagine the dragon is very, very small.*"

Adam pointed the dream doodler at the monstrous dragon, which now began rushing toward the children. It would be upon them at any moment! Adam shut his eyes and pressed the "DREAM DRAW" button.

"Look! The dragon's shrinking!" Zonia yelled.

And the dragon shrunk and shrunk and shrunk until it was no larger than a small rabbit.

A small wisp of smoke rather than the flickering flames now came from its mouth and nostrils. Rather than roaring dragon sounds, the tiny creature made only whimpering squeaks much like a mouse.

Toby rushed at the tiny dragon, which quickly scurried to a nearby hole in the earth. The children squealed and clapped while Toby dug at the hole into which the dragon had disappeared.

"It's okay, Toby," Adam said. "Leave him alone. Let's get out of here."

Soon the children stood on a flower-covered hill overlooking a tree-shrouded village. Adam held the sack of seven apples while he talked to Seth. "I guess you should give these to Grandfather Adam," he said.

"Grandfather Adam?" Seth questioned with a curious turn of his head.

"Oh…that's right. Grandfather Adam is *your* father, isn't he?"

Seth nodded *yes*.

"He is *my* grandfather," Enoch put in, looking into Seth's dark eyes.

"Actually, I think that Grandfather Adam is your great, great, great, great, great, great grandfather, or even more greats than that," Adam Beam said, glancing at Enoch.

It was all so confusing for the three boys.

"Since we are back in time from New Eden Time, and even back in time from Enoch's time, then that might make *you* Seth's..." Adam looked very confused. "...I don't know what that makes you."

"It doesn't make any difference," Zonia said with urgency in her voice. "We've got to get these apples to Grandfather Adam and then get back home."

A big butterfly flapped around Toby and landed gently on the tip of the tiger's broad nose. Toby's eyes nearly crossed trying to focus on the butterfly. Its fluttering wings made the cat sneeze.

The children all laughed as the butterfly flitted away. Toby rubbed his nose with one huge paw. Several of the children put their arms around Toby, petting him.

Adam said, "I don't know why these apples are so important, but you had better take them to Grandfather Adam...I mean your father...as soon as you can."

Seth started to take the sack of apples from Adam's hand when a dazzling burst of light brightened the whole hillside. Another 20-foot-tall figure of light appeared, this time standing between them and the village below.

"Slegna!" Seth said, moving back toward the children to protect them.

"No," Zonia said. "This is Zekor, our Lightons. There's nothing to be afraid of."

The tall, broad-shouldered being of light folded his arms and laughed joyfully. His golden eyes flashed rays of brilliant white light.

"That's right, little ones! There is nothing to be afraid of." The Lighton reached his shimmering hand down to pet Toby's head when the tiger bounded happily to him. "Good to see you, Mr. Toby!" the Lighton said with a roaring laugh that shook the whole hillside.

The children of Seth's time seemed to realize that Zekor was not from the Evil One, but from the Maker of All Things. They gathered around the Lightons, who knelt and welcomed them with open arms.

"You are all very, very brave children," he said, his golden eyes sparkling with love for them. "You have accomplished your mission wonderfully!" he said with more excitement. "Now the time is at hand for each of you to return to the time the Maker of All Things has purposed for you."

Toby snarled a snarl that seemed to say he understood the Lightons's words.

"Adam, you and your sister and Mr. Toby must return with Enoch to his time. You must take the seven apples with you."

The children said their good-byes to each other and to Toby. Enoch and Seth stood face to face, their eyes meeting in a moment of almost understanding.

"I have a grandfather who is named Seth," Enoch said quietly. "Do you think…"

The other boy said with equal softness in his voice, "I hope so, Enoch. I really hope so."

"I hope so, too," Enoch said with a smile.

"You must be on your way now," the Lighton said to Adam, Zonia and Enoch.

Within moments, a large dream drawing appeared in midair with Enoch already in it. Adam, Zonia, and Toby jumped through it and vanished

ADAM, ZONIA, AND TOBY STEPPED OUT OF THIN AIR and into Grandfather Adam's presence. Enoch was already standing there.

The old man jerked in surprise when the children popped through the Dream Door portal.

"We have returned, Grandfather," Enoch said, rushing to the old man and throwing his arms around his neck.

Zonia flung her arms around his neck and kissed his cheek.

"My little ones! Thank the Maker of All Things! You have come back to me safely!" he said, returning Zonia's hearty hug.

"These are for you, sir." Adam Beam said, holding the bag of seven apples outstretched toward Grandfather Adam. The old man hesitated for a moment, then with a broad smile and brightened eyes, reached to take the sack from Adam's hand.

He looked inside at the seven beautiful apples, and then at Adam. "It is a wonderful thing you have done, young one." He looked at Zonia and Enoch. "It is a wonderful thing that *all* of you have done."

Toby moved close to the old man and nuzzled against Grandfather Adam's leg.

"And you, too, of course!" Grandfather Adam said scratching the tiger behind his happily twitching ears. "Yes, Toby, you did a fine job, too!"

With Zonia sitting in Grandfather Adam's lap, he motioned for the two boys and Toby to gather around him. "Tell me all about your adventure. I want to hear *everything*!"

Zonia, with her eyes wide, almost told everything in one breath. Grandfather Adam listened with amazement. When Zonia had told everything she could think of, Adam Beam and Enoch filled in the details. Grandfather Adam was very pleased, indeed.

"My son told me that you children would return safely. And that you would bring the apples with you. The Maker of All Things is wonderful, is he not? Honor and praise and glory be to His name!"

Enoch said softly, quietly, "Is the son who told you that we would return safely with the apples my grandfather Seth? He is the boy named Seth in that long-ago time where we found the apples, is he not?"

"Yes," Grandfather Adam said, holding Enoch close. "It is your grandfather Seth who told me so."

The old man said to Adam Beam. "You have served the Maker's purpose well, young one. But your mission is not yet completed." Grandfather Adam handed the sack of apples back to Adam Beam. "You must take these with you when you return to your time and place."

The boy looked surprised.

"The purpose of the apples is for your time, not for my time. I know not what their purpose is. I only know that you are to take them with you. And may the Maker of All Things be with you!"

Good-byes were said and hugs were hugged. Grandfather Adam's great grandchildren took turns hugging and kissing and patting Toby, who snarled many snarls of happiness.

Adam's and Enoch's eyes met each other in silence for a moment. Enoch said, "I will very much miss you and Zonia and Toby."

Adam started to say something but stopped when he saw a white-haired man enter through a door. The man was old, but not as old as Grandfather Adam. He came to the boys and put his arms around them.

"This is my grandfather," Enoch said, glancing upward at the man who smiled down at the boys.

"His name is Seth?" Adam said, already knowing the answer.

Seth said, "It seems but a moment ago, my friend Adam. Somehow I know that this is not the end of our friendship, but that it is only the beginning."

* * *

ADAM, Zonia and Toby stood close together. Adam

held Zonia's hand. Zonia's other hand grasped Toby's thick fur.

"Farewell, little ones," Grandfather Adam said. All of the children chimed in, "Goodbye, Toby, Zonia, Adam!"

Adam Beam pushed the button marked "OUT" on the dream doodler's handle. Before the amazed Grandfather Adam, Grandfather Seth, Enoch and all the children, the air in the room began swooshing around Adam, his sister and the tiger. Faster and faster the air swirled with colored light. The hues spun and whirled faster and faster, and began to spark and flash. The air seemed charged with electricity as the lights became bolts of lightning that made crackling sounds that grew louder and louder.

"Wouldn't it be something to just disappear like that, and go to live with the Great King?" the wide-eyed Enoch said in a quietly amazed whisper, as if speaking only to himself.

Adam, Zonia and Toby revolved within the vortex. Around and around they turned, moving faster and faster through the spinning tunnel toward a pinpoint of blinding light that grew larger and larger.

Within seconds, the children's feet came to rest gently on the floor of the Exploretime cube. They were back in New Eden time.

Mrs. Levin's smiling face glowed with happiness. She hugged both children tightly and asked wasn't that a wonderful Dream Door Adventure!

Adam, just a bit shy about his Exploretime teacher making such a fuss over him while she kissed his cheek, looked down at his feet and smiled slightly without saying much.

Zonia, on the other hand, launched into a full wide-eyed telling of everything.

"And what is in the sack, Adam?" Mrs. Levin asked when Zonia had finished her amazing story of their Dream Door Adventure.

"Oh," Zonia said, "I forgot to tell you about Grandfather Adam telling us we must bring the apples back to New Eden time."

"These are Grandfather Adam's apples," Adam answered. "He told me they are for some great purpose." He repeated his sister's breathless explanation about the apples.

"For what great purpose?" Mrs. Levin said.

"We don't know," Zonia said enthusiastically. "Grandfather Adam didn't know, either. He just said that the Maker of All Things told him they were for some great future purpose."

"I see," Mrs. Levin said. "Perhaps the Brightons and the Lightons can help us with this wonderful mystery."

Adam held the sack containing the seven apples as tightly as anyone ever held a sack. He, his sister and Toby had brought the apples back through the swirling, whirling tunnels and passages of time, from ages and ages past to New Eden. Now he would hold onto the sack of apples with all his might until the Lightons or the Brightons told him about the seven apples' great future purpose.

Chapter 12

EVEN THOUGH BUD BEAM'S FAMILY WAS EXPECTING the Brightons visit, their sudden dazzling appearance in the kitchen startled Mr. and Mrs. Beam, and Adam and Zonia.

Brightons are much like the people of New Eden, except for their glowing brightness and their ability to walk through solid walls, or suddenly vanish without the help of a dream doodler. They have the ability to instantly travel to anyplace they chose, even to the farthest planet in the universe.

Brightons had once been humans, like the Edons. They once needed to eat food, and to sleep when they got tired. In the Before Time, old age, sickness and death were their enemies ... until the instant of the Great Taking Away when in a twinkling of an eye many humans of that Before Time had been changed into Brightons. Now they no longer grow old or get or sick. Like the Great King, they never die.

Adam Beam remembered the lessons he learned about the Brightons through Exploretime. The Brightons loved all of the children of New Eden, as did the Great King. Because they themselves were once children in the Before Time, Brightons always knew exactly how to make the children of New Eden Time happy. Brightons had invented the dream doodler with, of course, the blessings of the Great King.

Now the Brightons stood smiling down at Adam and Zonia. Toby rubbed against them as would a happy house cat.

One of the Brightons said, laughing and patted the big tiger between his ears. He said, "Adam, Zonia, we have come to you from His Majesty's throne. The Great King has sent us to summon you on the matter of your bringing the seven apples back from the first time. He is most pleased."

The Brighton's glowed brightened as he knelt on one knee in front of the two children and hugged them both. "Will you come tomorrow?"

The Great King! Why would anyone NOT want to go to the Great King? Both Adam and Zonia thought, their wide smiles and bright eyes giving the Brighton his answer even before Zonia spoke the answer for both herself and her brother.

"*QUANTUM!*"

Both Brightons laughed heartily at the little girl's expressive answer.

"I take it then that your answer is *yes?*"

"YES!" Adam and Zonia shouted almost at the same time.

Bud and Molly Beam beamed happily, seeing the happiness on their children's faces.

Toby didn't know exactly what it all meant, but he nevertheless snarled a pleased snarl, his long, thick striped tail brushing against and curling around the Brightons' legs while the tail swished back and forth.

"Be sure to bring the sack with Adam's Apples," the other Brighton reminded Adam.

* * *

ALL OF GLORAINIA had darkened with the veil of nighttime.

The great palace atop Mount Zonia sparkled. Adam Beam's father looked out Adam's bedroom window.

"Are you excited about going up to the Great Palace, Adam?" Bud Beam took one last glance out the window at the twinkly palace, then walked to Adam's bedside and sat on the edge.

"I can't wait!" Adam touched the sack with the seven apples sitting on the nightstand beside his bed. After all that had happened, he wanted to make sure the apples were safe. He must not disappoint the Great King.

"Dad…why do you think the Great King wants to talk to us?" he asked with just a little bit of worry in his voice.

"The Great King loves you, son. Whatever he wants to talk to you about, it will be wonderful!"

Mr. Beam reached to pull the covers up around Adam's neck, then bent to kiss him on the cheek. "You and your sister did a very fine thing by bringing the apples safely back with you. The Great King probably just wants to thank you."

"But the Great King deserves all glory and power and honor!" Adam said, amazed that anyone would not do the same to help the Great King. "The Great King deserves all praise!" Adam said, his heart full of love for the great King.

"That's true, son, and you and your sister have honored him greatly by bringing the apples safely to Glorainia," Bud Beam said, feeling very proud of his son's modest attitude.

Toby pushed Adam's bedroom door open with one big paw and walked over to the bed, where Mr. Beam was adjusting the covers for Adam. The tiger snarled a snarl that asked for a goodnight pat from his pal Adam.

Adam sat up, then grabbed the tiger's neck in a loving hug.

"Goodnight, Toby," he said, kissing the tiger's furry cheek.

* * *

THE GLORAINIAN MORNING broke as beautifully as ever.

Adam and Zonia ate their breakfast quickly, too

excited to even taste the wonderful honey oatmeal muffins from the manna manger. Toby ate only three fruitons and two huge helpings of catvage.

The kitchen suddenly filled with brilliant light, which lessened and lessened until Adam, Zonia and their mother could see clearly the Lighton whose head almost touched the kitchen ceiling.

He smiled widely, his golden eyes flashing and sparking powerfully. "Is everyone ready? I have come to personally take you to the Great King!"

Adam and Zonia sprang off their chairs. "Let's go," Adam said.

The Lighton laughed and gathered the children upon a shimmering cloud that suddenly formed between the Lighton's spread arms.

* * *

ADAM AND ZONIA rode safely upon the spinning cloud of bright white electricity. Faster and faster they flew, the colorful rolling ball of light beneath them sweeping them upward, ever upward toward Mount Zionia.

The great temple-palace radiated its own glow of many rainbow colors. So bright was its aura, the glow that pulsed from the Great King's palace, that Adam and his sister almost had to shut their eyes to look at it.

Magnificent streams of red, yellow, blue and every combination of those colors flickered and shimmered and sparked and flashed from the high walls made of diamonds and rubies and emeralds and other precious stone.

Zonia was mesmerized by the great temple's beauty. Adam blinked in amazement while he and his sister were whisked upon the rolling sparking cloud of energy toward the palace's high, massive gate of pure gold.

Just when it seemed that the Lighton's energy cloud would run Adam and his sister into the gate of solid gold, the monumental gate opened. The boy and girl riding in the Lighton's arms flew through the gate into the temple palace.

Never had Adam or his sister seen anything so wonderful! As magnificent as the outside walls of the palace were, the inside of the great temple sparkled even more gloriously. The bright cloud of energy flew the children more slowly inside the palace's shimmering walls. Finally, the fluffy rolling ball beneath them melted into a topaz mist and the Lighton gently placed each of the children upon the palace floor of gleaming gold. He held their small hands in his massive ones. "Let us go into the Great King," the Lighton said softly. Even so, his voice thundered within the great hallway.

A door as large as the palace gate and made of diamonds, rubies and emeralds, opened slowly and Adam and Zonia walked into the Great King's throne room.

Many Lightons, glimmering and glittering more brightly than the massive golden gates of the temple-palace, bowed before the throne. A crowd of

Brightons, their white robes glistening in the Great King's radiance, surrounded the King's throne.

The Lighton, holding the children's hands, stopped in the middle of the throne room and bowed on his knees before the Great King. The children, one on either side of the gigantic figure of light, bowed also toward the Great King.

Wonderful music, more beautiful than anything Adam had ever heard, seemed to come from the Great King's throne.

The Great King stood. The Lightons before the Great King's throne now formed a pathway while the Great King walked between them toward the children.

The Lighton who had brought them to the temple palace moved away from the children and joined the other Lightons.

Now the figure in dazzling white clothing stood over Adam and Zonia. The children were almost afraid to look at Him. When the Great King put His hands upon them, one on Adam and one on Zonia, all their fears melted away. In the place of fear they felt love beyond any love they had known before.

"Adam, Zonia. How wonderful that you have come to me!" the Great King said, bending to one knee in front of them and hugging them with gentle loving hugs. "We shall be the greatest of friends forever, my little ones."

Adam completely forgot about the sack of apples in his hand as he and Zonia looked into the Great King's soft eyes, filled with great love for them and for all the children of New Eden. They knew that indeed they could have no better friend than this Great King.

"You have done the most splendid thing for me, Adam, Zonia. Well done, my little ones. Well done, indeed!"

The Great King rose to his feet and, like the Lightons before him, took one of each of the children's hands in His hands and began walking slowly while He talked to them.

"Let us go and see what I have prepared for you. You will, I think, be quite pleased."

No one could possibly describe the indescribable things that the Great King prepares for those who love and serve Him. Therefore, it cannot be told the many wonders and the great joyfulness Adam, his sister, his mother and father, Mrs. Levin and Adam's Exploretime classmates celebrated with the King of all Kings that day.

And the very special guest of honor was, of course, Toby, who growled a growling roar of thanksgiving to the Great King.

The Great King stood in the midst of all those who celebrated with Him. The very air about Adam, his family and friends sparkled splendiferously with every color imaginable. The high, glittering, jewel-encrusted walls of the gigantic palace room reflected the brilliant rainbow display.

"Now there shall be a very blessed thing for you, my special friend, Adam," the Great King said, looking into the boy's eyes with love far exceeding any other. With one wave of His shimmering hand, the

Great King unveiled a viewing portal more spectacular than even the best dream drawing ever.

The rolling land in the dream drawing was New Eden, but even more beautiful that Adam ever remembered seeing it. The colors were brighter, the sky so crystal clear that even the stars shown during the day. And everywhere Adam looked, wonderful trees, the likes of which he had never seen before dotted the landscape. The sight of those trees reminded Adam of the sack of apples in his hand.

"These are for you," Adam said presenting the sack to the Great King.

The Greatest of all Kings to reign on any throne anywhere at any time took the sack from him and then lifted Adam from the palace floor with one arm while holding the sack of apples with His other hand.

"You and Zonia must join me at the throne this day. Together we have much to do!" He said.

The Brightons and Lightons, as well as all dignitaries of all of Glorainia and all of New Eden, bowed before the Great King. They all moved aside to clear a pathway to the great throne, which sparkled with every color imaginable.

When the Great King was seated, Adam and Zonia sat at the Great King's feet on the throne room floor of purest gold.

"Let this decree go forth," The Great King said, His eyes flashing, His voice booming with power and authority. "The seeds of the apples Adam the first man took from the garden of the First Time shall be planted throughout all New Eden!"

The Great King's words thundered and echoed not only in the glorious throne room but throughout Glorainia and all New Eden.

"All citizens of New Eden shall eat from the fruit of the seeds of the First Time. To do so is to live life everlasting and to know to do always good rather than evil."

The Great King's eyes softened as He bent to speak to the children. "Adam, Zonia, are you willing to do yet another deed for your king?" He said softly to the boy and girl.

"Yes, Great King," Adam and Zonia said at the same time rather quietly and shyly.

"Wonderful! The dream portal you just saw is a picture of what New Eden will look like in the future. The trees are those that you will plant."

Adam didn't know what to think. He had rescued Adam's Apples, and now he would plant the seeds in New Eden. It was almost too much for him to understand at that moment.

The Great King stood and His voice boomed throughout all of New Eden. "I hereby decree that my wonderful friends Adam and Zonia shall plant the seeds of the apples of the First Time tomorrow in Glorainia! The seeds from the apples of those trees shall then be sent to all of New Eden for the benefit of all Edons everywhere!"

Mr. And Mrs. Beam beamed brightly seeing the smiles on their children's faces. Toby, upon hearing the Great King's words, snarled a very, very pleased snarl.

Epilogue

EVEN DURING NEW EDEN TIME, DURING WHICH THERE is much goodness and happiness, evil yet lurks in the hearts of some New Edons. Usually those with evil in their hearts and mischief on their minds grow old more quickly than those with pure hearts and pure minds. Thus, with age on their faces at an early age, disobedient New Edons are known and swiftly judged under the Great King's perfect justice.

Two such Glorainians, Lester Mudd and Castor Groutt, listened with great interest to the Great King's proclamation.

Lester Mudd said, "They brought seven apples with them that came from the Garden of the First Time. Now they get to plant them in New Eden Time. It's not fair that Adam and Zonia should get all that glory."

"What can we do about it?" Castor Groutt said, pouting.

Lester thought a moment. "They took the apples from those Evols. I wonder how much money they'd pay to have them back?"

Castor blinked, and looked confused. "You want us to steal them apples from those two kids and sell 'em back to the evols?"

"Why not?" Lester said. He thought the idea had possibilities, but they had to act fast. Tomorrow Adam and Zonia would begin planting those seeds, and if they did, it would be too late to do anything about it!

Brighton

Supernatural people who were once natural people during The Before Time.

The First Time

The earliest time on Earth, sometimes called Antediluvian times.

The Before Time

The time on Earth that followed The First Time and was just before The Trouble Time

The Trouble Time

The time on Earth following The Before Time. It was a time when there were great and terrible wars and death unlike any other time.

New Eden Time

The time following the Trouble Time when all Earth is made new like it was in the beginning of The First Time, a time when The Great King reigns.

Catvage

A special tasty and good-for-tigers food that tigers can't resist.

The "Disappear Dazzler"

A button device on the Dream Doodler that makes people vanish when the button is pushed.

Dream Doodler

The almost miraculous instrument that children of the Kingdom Age use to imagine then draw scenes called Dream Doors.

Dream Doors

Beautiful scenes that hang in mid air when children use the Dream Doodler. These are portals of time and space through which children can then go to experience wonderful places and adventures that come from their own imaginations.

Evol

A spirit-like creature of the First Time that married humans of that time to produce offspring called Mutons.

Exploretime

The Kingdom Age education system for all children of New Eden.

Fruitonizer

The amazing machine that creates all manner of delicious fruits as if out of thin air.

Kingdom Age

The time on Earth that is gloriously new and beautiful, when The Great King reigns.

The Great King

The King of all Kings who rules all of New Eden.

The kindest, most magnificent King who ever was or ever will be.

Lighton

Creatures of brilliant light and immense supernatural powers who love and serve the Great King and Brightons.

Manna Manger

The marvelous food-producing machine that seemingly creates from nothingness the any meal people choose.

Muton

Hideously ugly and bad-tempered, 10-foot tall creatures that are the offspring of Evol and human intermarriage.

New Eden

Earth during The Kingdom Age.

Glorainia

The splendiferous capital city of all New Eden.

Slegna

Creatures of brilliant light and immense supernatural powers who chose the ways of evil rather than the ways of good.

The Wind Way

An unseen yet powerful sweeping wind that serves as an incredibly swift means of transportation from anywhere to anywhere in New Eden.

Zionia

The mountain towering high above Glorainia where sits The Great King's Temple Palace and His Throne.

A Look at Noah's Navy

The Millennial Kingdom is a wonderous time to be born into. The world is at peace and has become like the Garden of Eden; beautiful, exciting, and ruled by the Great King Himself who sits on His throne in the golden-street city of Glorania. In such a perfect place, who would expect thieves to prowl at night? It's those two fumblers again, Lester Mudd and Castor Grout. This time the troublemakers intend to steal a special gift entrusted to Adam Beam by the Great King. Luckily, Adam is startled awake during the burglary. Lester and Castor panic and escape through a carelessly drawn Dream Door, accidentally landing on Noah's Ark at the time of the Great Flood. It doesn't take Adam long to figure out where the thieves have gone. At once Adam, his sister Zonia, and their pet Siberian Tiger Toby are in hot pursuit to recover the stolen treasure, only to learn that the gift has fallen into the raging flood waters and is permanently lost.

Well, maybe not permanently. Adam has an idea how to find the precious gift, but it will take some clever Dream Doodling, the help of Noah and his family, a navy of friendly sea creatures, and . . . a submarine Dream Doodled from the far future. Naturally, the evil Evols intend to do all within their power to stop Adam from completing his mission.

AVAILABLE NOW FROM CKN CHRISTIAN PUBLISHING

About Douglas Hirt

Douglas Hirt was born in Illinois, but heeding Horace Greeley's admonition to "Go west, young man", he headed to New Mexico at eighteen. Doug earned a Bachelor's degree from the College of Santa Fe and a Masters of Science degree from Eastern New Mexico University. During this time he spent several summers living in a tent in the desert near Carlsbad, New Mexico, conducting biological baseline surveys for the Department of Energy.

Doug drew heavily from this "desert life" when writing his first novel, DEVIL'S WIND. In 1991 Doug's novel, A PASSAGE OF SEASONS, won the Colorado Authors' League Top Hand Award. His 1998 book, BRANDISH, and 1999 DEADWOOD, were finalists for the SPUR award given by the Western Writers of America.

A short story writer, and the author of twenty-nine novels and one book of non fiction, Doug now makes his home in Colorado Springs with his wife Kathy and their two children, Rebecca and Derick. When not writing or traveling to research his novels, Doug enjoys collecting and restoring old English sports cars.

About Terry James

Terry James is author, general editor, and co-author of numerous books on Bible prophecy, hundreds of thousands of which have been sold worldwide. James is a frequent lecturer on the study of end time phenomena, and interviews often with national and international media on topics involving world issues and events as they might relate to Bible prophecy.

He has appeared in major documentaries and media forums, in all media formats, in America, Europe, and Asia.

He appeared in the History Channel series, The Nostradamus Effect.

He is an active member of the PreTrib Research Center Study Group, a prophecy research think-tank founded by Dr. Tim LaHaye, the co-author of the multi-million selling "Left Behind" series of novels. He is a regular participant in the annual Tulsa mid-America prophecy conference, where he speaks, and holds a Question and Answer series of sessions on current world events as they might relate to Bible prophecy.

Terry James has been blind since 1993 due to a degenerative retinal disease (retinitis pigmentosa). He uses the Jobs Accessible Word System (JAWS) —which is voice synthesis—to write and conduct business over the Internet.

His former profession was in public relations, advertising, marketing, and publicity and promotion.

He received his education from Arkansas Polytechnic Institute, Memphis Academy of Arts, and University of Arkansas at Little Rock.

He served in both corporate and government positions for 25 years, before becoming a full-time writer.

James also served in the United States Air Force from October 1966 through October 1970.) He served at Randolph AFB, Texas, in the T-38 section, a mission dedicated to training pilots in high-performance jet fighter-trainers.

Terry James and his wife, Margaret, live near Little Rock, Arkansas.